I AM FRUIT OF THE EARTH

I AM FRUIT OF THE EARTH

ALDIVAN TORRES

Canary Of Joy

Contents

1 I am Fruit of the Earth   1

I

I am Fruit of the Earth

Aldivan Teixeira Torres
I am Fruit of the Earth

Author: Aldivan Teixeira Torres
©2018-Aldivan Teixeira Torres
All the rights Reserved
Aldivan Teixeira Torres

This book, including all its parts, is protected by copyright and don't can to be reproduced without author's permission, resold or transferred.

Short Biography: Aldivan Teixeira Torres, was born in Arcoverde, created the series the seer, the series sons of the light, poetry and screenplays. His literary career started at the end of 2011 with the publication of his first romance work Opposing forces – the mystery of the cave. For whatever reason, he stopped writing only resuming his career in the second half of 2013. Since then, he never stopped. He hopes that his writing will contribute to the Pernambuco and Brazilian culture, arousing the pleasure of reading in those that do not yet have the habit. His motto is "For literature, equality, fraternity, justice, dignity and the human being honor forever".

Dedication and thanks

I dedicate this book to the genuine owner of these Brazilian lands, which was named by the discoverers as an Indian. This outstanding character of our history made a great contribution to our culture in general, even in the face of the aggression and extermination of most of them. To them, my honor.

I thank first of all my good God for all the graces granted to my person and the nation, to my family always for being present in the good and bad moments, to my work colleagues for the motivation and companionship, my friends, the masters of life and teachers, to all who contribute in some way to a better world and especially to my readers. Without them, I am nothing. Keep going, always!

Introduction

I am fruit of the earth is a book that rescues our origins, a culture forgotten by the great majority. Entering a magical universe, we will discover the reason for some historical facts and the current reality of the Brazilian.

This is a book that inspires a reflection and a decision-making in front of the contradictory universe of our society. I wish everyone a good reading.

Summary

I am Fruit Of The Earth
Dedication and thanks
Introduction
Reencounter
The trip
Indigenous Society
Traditions, values, religiosity and art
Hypotheses of origin of the indigenous people
The colonization

Indigenous education
Health
State policies applied to natives
The Indians today
Indian movement
Citizenship, autonomy and indigenous gender
Worldview Tupi-Guarani
The various mythologies
Abaangui
Abaçaí
The sign of Andura
Angatupyry and Tau
The battle between the Carnijó and the Xukuru
A disastrous hunt
The boitatá
Boiúna
The meeting with the caipora
The legend of Pirarucu
The curupira
Legend of the sun and moon
Lara's spell
Ipupiara
Jurupari
Legend of the weed
The Legend of Victory-Regia
Maira
Pombero
Pytajovái
Saci pererê
Legend of Tamandaré
The creation according to the guarani mythology
The seven legendary monsters
The Xukuru people
Part II

Back from exile
Family on the river
Birthday
In school
The feast of the patron saint
The phone call
Change
Farewell

Reencounter

At the end of the adventure in Catimbau, our honorable characters have returned to their life as always in their routine of great commitments. Among the main ones were: Work in literature on other aspects, public service, work in the field, college studies, travel, social commitments, dealing with time and the anguish of a possible reunion. This was how they had felt since they met on that fateful crossing of the avenue in which one of them had almost lost his life and in the bucolic settlement of Jeritacó where they learned from one another to be masters of light.

The "Sons of Light" series was still very promising and the readers were eagerly waiting for another chapter of their stories. Without realizing it, the seer remained stagnant and occupied with other concerns. It was not easy to reconcile so many things at the same time and so it could be said that the same was forgiven. However, he was always open to a little push of fate.

Speaking of the little dreamer, he gets the release of his work to go to an event in his beloved Pesqueira town. It was the nineteenth day of April and on this date so important was celebrated Indian day in the Brazilian lands. Especially on this day, Divine felt connected to his native ancestors. It was like a call he could not refuse. To deny this would be something like rejecting his own blood.

After a lazy awakening, a bath, wearing typical clothes specially bought for that occasion, the use of social shoes and a good bath of perfume leave him prepared for what is to come. Being happy is this: A peculiar way of facing the world and challenges. The cave boy longed to live and these remarkable moments had to be enjoyed and celebrated.

Leaving his room already prepared, the son of God bids farewell in the living room of his relatives and announces his fast journey. His relatives, who always busy could not accompany him, receive the news naturally. All right, thinks the wittiest boy in the universe. Being alone was already part of his routine and taking a little air and meet new people would be very well for him. With optimism enough, our main idol waves, takes a few steps, opens the door, overtakes it and closes it, he walks a little on the porch of his house, he walks a little longer, and he passes the half-open gate straight towards the exit beyond his place. The next obstacle would be the tailgate of the property at about eighty yards from his abode. At this moment, the feeling is mild and he has quite a few expectations. Leaving home and going for a walk was something almost rare in his troubled life of chores. This little journey was the immediate solution so that he could improve his mood and his own vision of life. "It was always time to learn."

The rate increases slightly due to internal pressure and the hour itself. Wisely, at this time, was the attitude that was appropriate. However, on most occasions, patience is a key virtue for success. It is necessary to evaluate the needs on a case-by-case basis and this he had learned from experience and coexistence with the previous masters. No doubt, if anyone could not complain about enlightenment, this being was called Aldivan. Aware of this, he has no difficulty crossing the exit, closing the gate, passing the bridge, walk in the center of the village, and pass through the church, the square and reaching the lane. Luckily, an acquaintance passes by car; he stops and offers a ride to his destination. Without hesitation, he opens the door of the vehicle; he sits in the front seat and is given the start again. Towards the Pesqueira, the land of sweet and income. God bless them.

As soon as he got into the car, the friendly driver known as André Viçosa pulls in conversation.

"How's it going dreamer? All right? Are you off work?

"All good. Yes, I am. I will enjoy this day to go to Pesqueira. I have not been there in a long time. (The Seer)

"Good for you. How are the books? Have you sold enough?

"Nothing. What motivates me in the literature is not the financial question. The most important thing for me is the message and I will continue to convey something good to humanity. That's what God sent me to this place of atonement and testing.

"How cool. I wanted to know a little more about your work. Could you tell me a little about your books?

"It will be a pleasure. In the opposing forces, the first title in the series the seer, the book tells the story of a young dreamer who in a desperate attempt to realize his dreams, undertakes a trip to a mountain that promises to be sacred. He climbs it, overcomes obstacles and reaches its top. There, he meets the Guardian, a millenarian being holding almost all the mysteries and helped by her, he carries challenges accrediting him to enter in the mysterious and dangerous Cave of Despair (A sacred place that promises to realize the deepest dreams). Upon entering, he overcomes obstacles and finally he arrives at the Chamber of Secrets, where he becomes a seer, a gifted being. With everything accomplished, he leaves the cave and meets the guardian who sends him on an even more impossible mission - Gather opposing forces, solve injustices and help someone to meet. He accepts the project and, with his new powers, he takes a trip back in time guided by a distress call. The trip is a success and for 30 days is subjected to various adventures that make it take place. Back in his time, he celebrates his success. He promises to continue his mission, evolving more and more bringing entertainment to readers who follow him. Already in the second title, the dark night of the soul, life makes us live dark days, sorrows that we do not want to be real. "The dark night of the soul" is the sequel to "The Seer," and the main character returned to a mountain in search of answers to a troubled period of his life, moments that he had forgotten God, his principles, lost in sins. On the mountain, "The Seer" had contact with two "high beings", who guided him to knowledge. However, he is deeply connected to the seven deadly sins and in spite of the experience gained, his problems were not solved, having to make a journey to the "Lost Island", seat of the kingdom of the angels. This book is a crossing full of dangers, pirates, a great adventure at sea, bringing us reflections and questions, to which we wonder if it would be possible for a criminal to recover after sinking completely in the darkness, and, would he find peace for his crimes? Would he find forgiveness in himself? Would he find happiness? Or was it just an illusion, a truce for an even darker night? The third title is called the Encounter between two worlds, is a great journey of the adventurer's seer and Renato. It is divided into two parts that are situated in the past and the present respectively that seek to show the importance of the struggle for the realization of our ideals whatever they may be. In part one, I travel to the Place called Fundão to meet one of those responsible for a revolution in the past. Helped by him, the duo in question is trained to develop co-vision, key to the vision of history. When they are prepared, they are subjected to it and they travel to the early 20th century in the Northeast, time of oppression, injustice and prejudice and hunger. Throughout the time, they observe the example of the fighting population of the time, especially a group that takes an active part in the plot. However, have they had absolute success in their goals? Did they unmask the elites? Or they failed? And yet have they achieved the long-awaited meeting of worlds so disparate in relation to social classes, opinions, stereotypes and love? It is worth checking. In part two, the pair make a new trip with the goal of completing their work and achieving the miracle so sought after. This time, they go to Carabais to look for a second personage of the past and when they find it, they are put under new training. When ready, part two of the story shows. In it, the reader will face the following questions: To what extent does the social issue hamper success? Is it feasible to persist even after several failures? Is it worth depriving yourself of love because of prejudices without even trying? Can anyone who has a gift consider themselves special or can this be crazy? All this and much more you will see in the story of Divine, someone in search of the destiny and the success that we all deserve. Regarding the fourth title, The Testament God's Code, the story begins when Philip

Andrews, an auditor of the farm marked by a tragedy, begins to wonder why his bad fate become revolted and outraged. By a bid of fate, he discovers a book and an author and decides to look for it. When meeting him with his adventure partner they decide to take a trip to the distant desert where they supposedly would meet God and solve their problems. The trip is then accomplished, finding two guides on the way that lead them to the desired location, Cabrobó desert. Passing through ten cities in the desert, they develop a hearty chat with each other and their guests and suddenly God begins to speak through the guides answering crucial questions. Everything that is revealed helps in the elaboration of the "testament", a code given by God and never deciphered in human and angelic history. What's up? Do you believe that God can reveal Himself in extreme situations? Or is it just a delusion from everyone involved? Read the testament, a book intended especially for those who have lost faith in God, and draw their own conclusions. In the fifth title, I am, are thirteen stories, a dreamer, a young man and two archangels in search of the truth. What has in common a depressive, a pedophile, an abortionist, a drug addict, a professional player, scientists, criminals, a sexologist, a schizophrenic and a handicapped person? Both seek to reflect on their actions, their future directions alongside the seer, a revolutionary and special being, on a great journey in northeastern Brazil. Declaring himself the son of God, he promises to listen to everyone, advise them and give valuable tips on how to resume life by showing his personality and father over time. The ultimate goal of all is to awaken the inner self of each of them and attaining this miracle the truth will be revealed at last. "I am" also represents a cry of freedom in the face of social conventions as in the past. "I am" is shown in this way how truly the human being is at odds with those who are accustomed to judge others. A thought-provoking and promising book. Already in the sixth, War in the skies, it is the sixth epic journey of the series team the seer. The plot is developed on the planet Kalenquer, dimensional portals, ancient and present São Paulo. In the first part, it brings like content the great universal war, the war of the angels, and the pertinent reflections. In the second, a deepening of the prejudices that today cause an implied war on humanity. The purpose of the book is to discover a little of destiny, our history, the current reality of human society and invites us to take the lead in our decisions and who knows how to change old paradigms. It is only enough to want to follow the commandments of Yahweh and then the impossible will become possible. These are the six books published so far in the series "The Seer". I still have many other titles. In the poetry genre, "Reciting the love" is a set of poetry with main background love, this strong and enduring feeling that many have already experienced. In the text, we have the profound revelations in the most varied contexts applied to this genre. I hope these writings contribute even more to the poetic and loving world. The second title, Verses from the countryside, talks a little about the typical regional elements of the Northeast. In this genre were these two titles. I also have, Parables of the kingdom and of wisdom, a compilation of tales surrounding the wisdom and kingdom of God. Invitation Wisdom is a collection of phrases in the proverbial style. Destiny is a brief account of my life bringing important learning. Book Synopsis: We all have a mission, some with bigger ones and some with smaller ones. The important thing in this is to have a positive attitude towards life even if the obstacles are enormous. Destination comes to bring a little of Divine, a young Northeast who grew up in the face of the challenges of a dry, poor and prejudiced region. The example of Divine can be inspiring so that you do not give up easily of your dreams. So, what to expect to know Divine? A good reading and success in your endeavors. The two paths present the opposing faces of good and evil. In life, we have two choices. Knowing how to choose one of them is a matter of wisdom. Learn to reflect on this with a young man who has the predicates for such and who can point out solutions to common indecision problems in life. Christians bring hope. Many unmotivated and unguided people live by asking themselves what the meaning of life is in the face of an increasingly cruel world. The Christians come to bring that little bit of encouragement, guiding and advising on the most diverse aspects of life leading us to a deep reflection. When you finish reading the text, the goal is for the person to change their pace of life and be happier. To win by faith brings good reflections. Life is really a Ferris wheel: One day you are at the peak of success and happiness and in the other, you can fall into disgrace. In these difficult times, the most important thing is to keep the faith in a larger force and try to rebuild. Seeking to win by the power of faith is the ideal to resume the routine and the promise of better days. Believe it is possible! The word revealed is a set of texts that aim to make explicit the various questions of life. Inspired by God, these short thoughts will inspire you to make important decisions that will lead you to the right path. It will be a balm for the soul troubled and weary of the inclemency of life. From weakness comes strength to bring the breath to distressed and troubled souls. Life is made of phases. Knowing how to extract from pain the experience you need to move forward and win is what few know. Discover the secret of success. In relation to the just and the relationship with Yahweh, it is a tale focused on religiosity. This tale brings practical advice in the relationship with the parent and encourages optimism and perseverance. If you are in a difficult time this is the best time to read it and resume your hopes. Sophia is the soul of God raised to the point of touching the human heart. Through slight strokes, the purpose of the story is to elucidate the main topics so that the human soul can finally realize how important it is. In the Law of Return, in this life we only have what we deserve and what we sow. To know how to live with it and to act in order to succeed is what few know. Know a little of this universal law. Lastly, the series "Sons of Light have two titles published." The voices of light are the first book from Series "Sons of light", series whose main theme is religious and relationships between people. It aims to inform, reflect, question values and put ourselves before historical facts. I invite the reader to delve deep into this adventure full of entertainment, mystery and information that will certainly contribute to a new vision of life and future. With compliments, feel free. The second, Bruised Wounds, brings some of the pain we have gone through and ways to live with it. We all carry important marks of pain and discouragement in the face of life's events. What to do with this is what many people ask themselves. Wounded brands come to bring a script and at the same time answers to their most disturbing inquiries. It is a highly recommended book for those who have not yet found the path to happiness. These are my published titles.

"Wow! Over? They're a lot. Congratulations! I'll want them all.

"Thank you. It's almost three years of dedication and I'm very proud of it. In a while, the difficulties were so many that I gave up. Now I am determined to persevere in the way. Wish me luck.

"Of course. From what I see, you have a lot of talent. Do not rush. Your time will come.

"Amen!

"And what about the love? I do not see you with anyone.

"I don't even want to talk about that. This is a callous in my life. Despite being beautiful, hot, intelligent, loving and caring I do not receive reciprocal from anyone. Nowadays it is very complicated to love so much that I have already lost hope. If there is a light at the end of the tunnel, I do not know. Maybe one day.

"Who knows? I've known you all along. You're a really nice guy. You certainly deserve to be happy. I'll always be cheering.

"Thank you very much.

Without realizing it, tears flow over the suffered face by the seer, the most respected guy in the world. Talking about it made him very ill because of unpleasant circumstances not worth to remembering. André realizes this, an uneasy silence hangs between them, and the journey continues. The moment had to be respected.

Going forward, our two friends advance on the busy highway BR 232. On the way, they pass by the Climério site, Novo Cajueiro, Ipanema and Canaã. They do not return to the embarrassing subject because it represented "the wounded marks" of the illustrious dreamer. It needed time and patience so they could get more answers. Meanwhile, it was up to them to fulfill their role in the unfolding of the plot. What would become of them? What did destiny point to in the future in relation to your expectations? What reaction could this entail? The many unanswered questions seemed to foresee a hidden, mysterious, undefined, yet comforting side. Whatever it was, they were fully prepared. At least that is how they felt.

On the one hand was a married man, father of three beautiful children and a dedicated wife. His goal was to consolidate their relationship and stay alive. On the other side was the cave boy, single, employed, writer, almost accomplished, with a consolidated family and his own ethical values. Among his many aspirations were a marriage to someone legal, to be on his professional side, to pass on a good message to the universe in order to conquer the world. The promise of the superior spirits is out in a moment when nothing was right. This time is called the dark night, a time when the human being disconnects from God and thinks only of his vanities. Fortunately, this period passed and by a miracle our idol was saved. The merits of this fact are unique to his father, Yahweh, who through his angel touched the heart of this suffering man causing him to reconsider an important decision. It was only for very little that he had not fallen into a deep, dark pit. Thanks to this miracle, he promised to change and he found in his spiritual father the support needed to find a new path. He is now very happy with his work, with his family, and with himself. He did not have everything, but whatever came was credited as a promise. Faith, a small word, but with an incredible power of change. So were the days of these special characters.

Specifically, on the trip, they are already approaching the Pesqueira center. The conversation is resumed on general subjects with the intention of distraction. The atmosphere is good with plenty of expectations. André would find distant relatives and the son of God would go to an event commemorating that important day for Brazilians. About to mark history in their trajectories, both prepared mentally and spiritually with purpose to find answers, to learn and to experience new experiences. It was time to change the routine and embark on an unforgettable adventure. They would be kept in a special little corner of the heart of readers scattered all over the world. No matter what role they play, big or small. As they say in slang, they would "Cause".

Encouraged by this possibility, the car's march is accelerated and then they can already glimpse "The Rough Princess". The Pesqueira of all of us was a pleasant, historic city, home to an intellectualized, hard-working people, yet suffered much hope for a better future. One of these illustrious children was a young man published in various countries who preached love, freedom, tolerance, equality, peace, harmony, cooperation, charity, simplicity and forgiveness. It was a challenge to live in a world so different from his conception. However, challenges were made to be overcome.

A few minutes later, they already have access to the central, first Pesqueira district. The opportunity makes the seer remember his trajectory just when he was making this journey every day in search of fulfilling his public function. Good times those! For almost four years, he served administrative duties at Christ the King College assisted by helpful co-workers. His departure from this establishment was due to approval in another public function better remunerated. Although he never forgot his origins, it was the best decision in terms of personal need. As the saying goes, absolutely nothing is forever. The Seer would continue to search for more experiences in every way. Crossing the central, revisiting places, passing through the center they go against the main point of the city, the Plaza Dom José Lopes. There, it's the farewell place between the two friends and Andre would go his own way. Now the son of God mingles with the crowd, coming closer to the main stage of the party. There is a presentation of Toré, typical dance of the Xukuru Indians. Divine had never witnessed such a peculiar and folkloric spectacle. He concentrates so hard he barely notices it when someone touches his back. Turning back, what a surprise to see two old friends. After the complimentary kisses and hugs, they begin to communicate with each other.

"My God! What a surprise. What are you doing here, my dear friends? (Aldivan)

"We came to the solemnity and to meet a friend. (Reported Messiah)

"I'm glad we had this award from God. How have you been, Son of God? (Emanuel)

"Well, in my usual routine. I'm taking more care of the trucks. (Divine)

"I know. I also do not forget that fateful day. The unpleasant fact served to unite us and to initiate the series "Children of the light". Nothing is by chance in this world. (Emanuel observed)

"It is true. Do you appreciate indigenous art? (The son of God)

"Yes, a lot. I have several friends in the area and the main one is here in this presentation. Look, that tall, thin old man located in the center of the stage - Pointing with a finger to the man (Messiah)

The man smiles. He recognizes the old schoolmate in the crowd. But who were the two young men who accompanied him? He felt a strong vibration and protection in them. Earth spirits try to communicate by predicting something. However, everything is very confusing. It would be best to wait until the end of the presentation to close your doubts or even increase them.

"I know, I saw it. It's a very interesting guy. It will be a pleasure to meet him. (The Seer)

"You will not regret. He is dope. (Messiah)

"Dope? Do you know anything about Emanuel? (Divine)

"I'm more lost than you, because I do not know him either. In fact, I did not even know of his existence. Suddenly, my father had this idea to come to Pesqueira and rescue this story. To conclude, destiny united us again. (Emanuel)

"I know. I'm putting things together: Indian day, the three of us gathered here and a mysterious stranger to know. It could be what was missing for a new story. Am I right, master? (Aldivan)

"Maybe. The presentation looks beautiful, does not it? (Messiah responded trying to dislodge)

"Yes. (Little Dreamer)

"It's all beautiful. (Emanuel)

Aldivan does not require explanations. Something he had learned from himself was to be patient and recognize the moment of each thing. Simply the best was to be enchanted by the rhythmic movements of the artistic group. The future was still something to be built and required time and dedication.

The trio takes advantage of every moment of that magical moment to enjoy the beauties of our culture. There were martyrs, sufferers, strugglers, heroes, dreamers and Brazilian citizens in their broadest sense. At the end of the presentation, they go to the dressing room to greet the artists and rediscover the person mentioned. They were satisfied, happy, confident and hopeful. Everything could change as if it were magic and completely transform the lives of those musketeers. The field of possibilities was enormous and fully possible.

Climbing up the stairs that led to the stage, our friends tremble inside, unable to control the emotion whose revelation was about to take place. What awaited them? What decisions could be taken from there? The only certainty they had was that they were willing to go even further down that mysterious path.

Fully committed, our fellow adventurers have access to the top of the stage and from there does the master previously appoint just a few steps to the man's dressing room. They knock on the small green doorway located right in the center of the building. Immediately, they hear footsteps and a few moments later the seemingly sympathetic elder attends them. Wearing a silk blouse, jeans, sunglasses, green cap with the Brazilian flag symbol, black social shoes and emanating an unmistakable jasmine scent, the man looked nothing like what was expected of a native of an Indian tribe. With a fraternal gesture, he greets everyone and very excited begins to pull conversation:

"My great friend Messiah. What a pleasure to see you again after many years. Who are your companions?

"It is a great pleasure, too, my dear friend Juraci. These are my son Emanuel and my friend Aldivan - Pointing to each of them. (Emanuel)

"Welcome, I hope you're well and well-behaved - Juraci said.

"Thank you. My father has revealed a little of your history on this important day that is yours, the genuine Brazilians. (Emanuel)

"It is an honor to be here participating in this unique moment. (The Seer)

"Actually, I brought them with ulterior motives. I meditated a little and guided by my guides I arrived here in Pesqueira. I want you to teach us everything you know. (He requested Messiah)

"It's time? I really am impressed by the quality of the energy I receive from You. The Xukuru path is not easy, it's a challenge every single step on the ground. However, as mother earth I am always available to open my arms and welcome them. Do you want to be trained? No problem. Your friend is here to serve you on your intriguing journey of adventure. (Juraci)

"Great. (Messiah)

"Where shall we go? (The Seer)

"To my house and your house, besides the foot of Ororubá mountain. Do you have availability? (Juraci)

"I'll check. Wait a second. (The son of God)

The seer moves away and calls from his cell phone. The goal is to get a work permit and communicate to the family his decision. In about five minutes, he gets both feats. There was nothing to stop him from following his course. He then returns to his colleagues.

"I agreed. I have the time. I am very interested in the question of your people. I am your disciple from now on and I promise dedication, readiness, courage and faith. (The Seer)

"Very good. Is that okay with you, Emanuel? (Juraci)

"It's all right. Let's go together in this new adventure! (Emanuel)

"Then follow me. (Juraci)

The trip

The group leaves the dressing room, enters the chartered car, leaves the center and travels a good part of Pesqueira until reaching the lane towards the village. From the beginning, they feel the difficulties of the road. The best way to pass the time is to talk and observe the horizon. That's what they do. The climb up the mountain was long and they were amused by their new friend's jokes. Despite his age, he was quite cheerful and willing. Without doubt, great wisdom was enclosed in that heart perhaps wounded by the problems of life. Everything for our friends was new: the relief, the vegetation, the clean air, the hot sun, the intense ascent, the dangerous curves and the nervousness that was great. But it was all worth it.

Advancing in the same conditions, they arrive at the village of Cimbres and soon after in the main village. The agglomeration is composed of simple houses made of crossed sticks and clay with ceramic roof. Juraci's house was the last and also the simplest. At first, they settle and go to rest. Afterwards, as arranged, they had a meeting so that they could get to know each other better and delimit their work. It is held still in the morning and below has the main passages of the conversation:

"I am the Juraci I am the fruit of the land of this thriving wild Pernambuco. I was born and raised in these lands and I learned from an early age to preserve and respect them. And you? What is your testimony?

"My family comes from Europe, but I also consider myself Brazilian. Brazil has always welcomed me well despite the fact that we did not have sufficient conditions to survive in a dry northeast with no opportunities. This is the best place in the world to live by the challenges imposed by the intelligence, goodness and willpower of its people. I am proud to be here, to be the Messiah, the master of the light who seeks answers with an old friend.

"I am Emmanuel, the one who came to save. My attitude freed the young dreamer and with him I could understand a little more of God. I live in the backlands with my father and I'm here to participate in this complex teaching-learning system.

"I am Aldivan Teixeira Torres, also known as son of God, seer, Divine or little dreamer. I'm a civil servant and writer. My greatest achievement was to defeat the most dangerous grotto in the world and to have succeeded in the various adventures already completed so far. Nowadays, I intend to take advantage of this wonderful moment to absorb the necessary knowledge. Where did you know beloved teachers?

"I've been away from my tribe because of political dissent. I met Messias on a farm near Ibimirim where we worked together in manual activities. We were still children and spent much of our childhood together. When the situation finally changed, I returned to my people and we did not see each other so often. (Juraci)

"Those good times. We suffer greatly from the impiety and indifference of the greatest, but we create a bond of friendship so strong that it unites us to this day. On this special day, every Brazilian day, I had this great idea to review it. Then we take advantage of your wisdom so that we can evolve and get to know new cultures. (Messiah)

"Perfect. I am available. What are your goals beyond this? (Juraci)

"To live. My retirement gives me some financial security being a trophy for my effort throughout my life. I want to go further. (Messias)

"I want to get married, get a steady job, keep participating in this wonderful series and travel a lot. (Emanuel)

"I want to move forward with my literary career, arousing the pleasure of reading in those who do not yet have this habit. The ultimate goal is to conquer the whole world. I also want to be happy in one way or another. Knowledge is everything. (The son of God)

"Very well. For my part, I want to fulfill my mission. I do not know if I have much knowledge as they say, I know what nature taught me. I will be another arrow in your path. (Juraci)

"What's the first step? (The Seer)

"I'll do a special training where you will learn about the specificities of my people. The goal is to become worthy for the ultimate revelation. The first stage will be held in the afternoon. For now, let us rest. Now I'm going to take care of lunch. (Juraci)

"It's ok. (Aldivan)

Juraci retires to fulfill the agreed and our friends enjoy going out and get to know the village better. On the tour they meet more people and get in touch with them. Contrary to popular belief, the Indians are kind and friendly people, they do not look like old descriptions of violence and shamelessness. They are also friendly, welcoming and owners of a valuable culture. It would be very worth the trip.

After touring virtually every corner of the place, our musketeers resolve to return to the home of their dearest friend Juraci. At this very moment, they were aware of their desires, limitations, the range of possibilities ahead, gravity and danger in the way of the wisdom of the ancients. However, they were accustomed and ready to take the risk.

Perfectly aware, they walk step by step the small route from one end of the village to the other. Since everything there was small, it does not take long and they already complete the total route. And now? What would happen? Their anxiety and nervousness were enormous in the face of life's unknowns. Pushing the door, they already smell the local food. Judging by the smell, it must have been a delight. With a wave, the host calls them to sit on the small wooden table in one of the corners of the hut.

One by one, they approach and settle around the furniture in small stools carefully distributed in the small space. Even with the humility there, they were happy because they were among friends. This rule applies to life situations. What good is living in a mansion being unhappy and lonely? What's the use of having money and not having health? It is preferable to be poor, healthy and have trusted people who truly love you. Another thing: Knowledge is measured by experience and sensitivity having nothing in common with power, social status, religion, political power or prestige. In general, evolved souls reside in social littleness.

The food is served. Given the expectations, the host's prepared chicken stirring is fine. As they eat, they enjoy interacting with each other.

"How are your expectations regarding this adventure? (Juraci)

"The best possible. I believe that we are part of a new history where friendship and unity of all will be fundamental. (The Seer)

"Staying here is like a great historical dive. Although we are in the 21st century, I feel all the climate of the past. This is very constructive. (Emanuel)

"Everything tends to improve and to know this culture so important is fundamental. (Messiah)

"Very well. I'm glad you are so willing. You know, I must confess that I've never trained anyone. All I know comes from the nature and reports of my people, which I have access to. But if I have the confidence of my old friend Messias, I will strive to serve them. (Juraci pronounced)

"Certainly. Thanks for the support. (Messiah)

"We are convinced of your ability. It will be very fruitful. (The son of God)

"Great men reveal themselves in little things. (Emanuel)

"Good words. It seems like a dream to have this chance of life. I promise not to disappoint you. (Juraci)

"Amen! (The others)

The conversation went on for a little more time on other subjects. So far, everything was going very well on the trip to that sanctuary. In the future, they might have the desired answers to their aspirations if they fully assimilated the planned steps. Self-confidence was not lacking in our friends.

At the end of lunch, they meet again and unanimously they decide to leave. They pack necessary belongings because the goal was to stay in the woods of the mountains for a few days. All the learning would unfold there. With everything ready, they begin the short walk.

From the village, they take a trail to the east, and from the beginning, they feel some difficulties. The relief was extremely rugged and the forest very closed. Dangerous thorns, pointed stones, and wild animals further complicated the situation. However, no one complains. On the contrary, they appreciated the experience of that moment.

With a regular walk, they gradually overcome obstacles and fears. The current thinking was of cooperation, delivery, dedication, courage and faith that overcame doubts and worries. In the end, one was expected to realize the greater goal: To know yet another voice that had shouted in the grotto of despair.

In about forty minutes of walking, they find the perfect place to camp. It was a relatively flat, spacious place with trees all around and almost in the center of the forest. Their first action is to build a shelter. With the help of the experienced Indian, they seek wood and straw in the woods. When returning, each one contributes in his own way to raise the hut. She stands firm and protects them from sun, rain and dangerous animals.

With everything accomplished, it is time for the first debate of ideas.

Indigenous Society

"Begin with the questions about our society. I'll be ready to respond. (Juraci was available)

"What do the Indians live for? (Emanuel)

"Hunting, fishing, livestock, agriculture, handicrafts and the income of indigenous federal programs. (Juraci)

"What do you plant? (The Seer)

"A little of everything. The most common products are: Maize, beans, pumpkin, sweet potato and cassava. (Juraci)

"What way do the plantations do? (Messiah)

"We use the coivara, felling of forest and burned to clear the soil for planting. (Explained Juraci)

"Interesting and rudimentary. We did it like this in the old days. Today we plowed the land before planting. (Messiah)

"We, the Indians are very attached to the tradition inherited from our ancestors. (Juraci)

"Do you drink? If so, what kind of drinks do you produce? (The Seer)

"We do. We have extensive knowledge in the production of fermented beverages made from tubers, roots, leaves, seeds and fruits such as corn, cassava, sweet potato, cashew, peanut, banana and pineapple. (Juraci)

"Can we say we inherited this custom from you? (The son of God)

"Exactly. (Affirmed Juraci)

"And in cooking, what do we inherit from you? (Emanuel)

"Foods based cassava and maize taking as an example the mush and tapioca. The use of guarana, Palm heart, sweet potato, pinhão, cocoa, peanut, caruru, serralha, papaya, araçá, caju, abajeru, apé, araticum, azamboa, bacaba, bacupari, grumixama, guapuronga, mocurí, mundururu, murici, ubucaba and umari. In relation to food derived from animals, we have turtle and its eggs such as arabu, abunã, mujanguê and paxicá; of fishes, we have the paçoca and the moquém, the piracuí, the moqueca and the mixira. (Juraci)

"Almost all of this I love. Thank you very much. (Emanuel)

"You're welcome. (Juraci)

"say other related contributions. (Requested Messiah)

"We introduced other vegetables such as cotton fibers, tucum, grasses, bamboos and wild guarana for the manufacture of fabrics, ornaments and basketry; to make brooms to palm fiber; Genre's pumpkins to produce gourds, used to store water or flour. (Juraci)

"Very instructive. (Messiah)

"How about the animals? (Emanuel)

"In our reserves, we domesticate the ox, horse, donkey, goat, chicken, pig among others and we use them in our food, transport and what we spare we sell. (Juraci)

"Well, modern. And formerly? (Emanuel)

"According to writings, we knew only small animals. (Juraci)

"How about hunting? (The Seer)

"We catch wild animals of various species to help feed. We have been great hunters ever since. (Reported Juraci)

"And you guys think it's right? End the life of these animals for your own benefit? (The Seer)

"Do not get me wrong, but what do you whites do? You destroy the vegetation, exploit the animals, deplete the earth's ores, kill, steal, and usurp our lands. We act differently: We respect the land and the animals by taking only what is necessary for our survival. So, do not give me a moral lesson. (Said angrily Juraci)

"Sorry, you're right. We whites are to blame for the current land degradation situation. (The son of God)

"Still, that is wise. Forgive me if I was thick. (Juraci)

"No problem. (Aldivan)

"Like a good Indian, our friend here loves fishing, does not he? (Messiah)

"Yes, we have several lakes and rivers in this region and fishing is a form of leisure and past income from generation to generation. Not even the acculturation imposed by white has taken away this characteristic. (He observed Juraci)

"Very good. I'm from an Italian family, but I also love fishing. We have similar tastes. (Messiah)

"It's true, my friend. (Juraci)

"How do you communicate with the other Indian tribes? (Emanuel)

"We use the whole modern apparatus: Telephone, internet and post office. On important dates, we gather and celebrate. (Reported Juraci)

"And in the past? (Emanuel)

"We sent messengers to warn about important matters. In general, when it came to times of wars, marriages, burial ceremonies and also when establishing alliances against a common enemy. (Explained Juraci)

"Got it. (Emanuel)

"What about the use of natural resources? (The Seer)

"We use right everything that mother earth offers us. From the wood we build canoes, bows, arrows and our houses. From the straw we make baskets, mats, nets among others. The pottery is used to make pots, pans and household utensils. Feathers and skins are used to make clothes or decorations for our ceremonies. Urucum is used to make paintings on the body. Our women also make renaissance by contributing to the local economy. (Juraci)

"Hum, very ingenious. You are to be congratulated. (Aldivan)

"Grateful. (Juraci)

"In relation to social classes. How do you organize yourself? (Messiah)

"There are no social classes between us. All are equal. The land is common property and when we harvest or hunt, we share it all. Selfishness is something we do not know. The only property we have is our personal belongings. (Juraci)

"How does the division of labor occur? (Messiah)

"We divided by sex and age. Women are responsible for food, handicrafts, children, harvesting and planting. Men, on the other hand, take care of hunting, fishing, farming, and cutting down trees. (Juraci)

"Well fair. In the white world it's a bit different. Nowadays, the attributions of man and woman are very similar. (Messiah)

"I know. That is why the women of our tribe and even the white women worship us. (Juraci)

"Truth. (Messiah)

"What are the main characters in a tribe? (Emanuel)

"It's the shaman and the chief. The shaman is the religious figure of the tribe because he knows the rituals and receives the messages of the spirits. He also acts as a healer knowing the teas and herbs to cure diseases. The cacique guides and organizes the Indians. (Juraci)

"How is the family constituted? (Messiah)

"In relation to marriage, the family may be monogamous or polygamous with a predominance of polygamy. Marriage is not a sacred institution with divorce being frequent. There are many consanguineous unions, which strengthen the unity of the clans. Each family and its relationships are considered private. The mother breastfeeds the small child until there is no other child. If he is a boy, the father teaches him his work. In the same way, if is a girl, the mother teaches the feminine activities. There are rituals in specific periods being celebrated by the whole tribe. (Juraci)

"A little different from our white culture. (He observed Messiah)

"Very different. Each one has its importance. (Juraci)

"How about we shift focus a little? (The seer inquired)

"Of course, it can be. (Juraci was available)

"Let's talk a little about your culture. (Aldivan)

"You can start. (Juraci)

Juraci's disposition was impressive despite his age. The conversation was very good and would continue until they were completely satisfied.

Traditions, values, religiosity and art

"The cosmos for most humans and me is a mystery. We have so many theories, but none of them satisfy us. How do your people see this mystery? (The son of God)

"For us, the world did not have a defined origin or purpose. Some of us believe in a supreme God having the help of secondary Gods. For others, the origin of the world is a mystery, and various myths arise to wise heroes and benevolent entities. There are also cosmogonies with a pair or a collectivity of breeders.

"Very interesting. In my belief, God was there at the beginning triggering the explosion designated by science as Big Bang. Children, angels, and all other civilizations were created. God has always existed and will never die. He is the reason of my life. (The son of God)

"Splendid. From the beginning, I realized the good energy coming from you. Although I have different beliefs, I firmly believe what you say. (Juraci)

"Thank you. I also respect your culture. (Divine)

"You are special. (Juraci)

"That is why he's the son of God. I have the honor of saving your life once. He is in good hands. (Emanuel)

"I was his master and his disciple, and both times, it was very fruitful. That is why I brought you here and I see that was the best decision. (Messiah)

"How nice. I am glad. Let us continue our learning. (Juraci)

"Could you tell us the relationship between the nature and the religiosity of your people? (Messiah)

"Animism is recurrent, that is, the deification of various animals, plants, mythological beings, the earth and its elements. We consider all this sacred. There is also a belief in unfathomable divine power linking nature and men. For us, there are countless dimensions and in certain situations they communicate with each other in the great chain that is life.

"That is why there is this relationship of respect between you and nature. Making it spiritual is a great strategy. (He observed Messiah)

"This is our choice. Man is a thread of nature and the preservation of it is fundamental for life to continue. Too bad the white man does not think so. (Juraci)

"Truth. Our greed will still lead us to ruin. (Messiah)

"Something that caught my attention was the idea of parallel worlds. This belief reveals much wisdom from you. I also believe in multiple universes. The proof said is that my friends and I already live several situations in alternative worlds. (Aldivan)

"You are lucky. To deny the spiritual burden of the other worlds is the same as stumbling in one's own legs. However, not everyone is prepared. (Juraci)

"This is true. (The Seer)

"What conceptions do you have of postmortem? (Emanuel)

"There is a belief in a paradise for the good and the brave. We perform burial rituals in order to preserve their memory. (Juraci)

"In our culture there is heaven, hell, limbo, the city of men, and purgatory. Heaven, purgatory and the city of men for the faithful and other places for the bad ones. (Emanuel)

"We believe in good and evil too. So much so that we protect ourselves against disorderly spirits through rituals. (Juraci)

"They do well. In our culture, the action of evil happens through work using black magic. People are bad. (Emanuel)

"I know how it is. (Juraci)

"It is written that those who seek evil will not inherit my kingdom. I want the humble, the small and the good-hearted. (The seer affirmed)

"Do we, wild Indians, have a chance to enter your kingdom? (Juraci)

"The door is open for everyone. Just believe in my name, my father's, and do good works. As the saying goes, there are many ways to reach God. (The Seer)

"Amen. Good. (Said Juraci relieved)

"What differentiates the indigenous religion from the others? (The Seer)

"There is no specific dogma or liturgy, much less scripture. We respect all beings being unacceptable sacrifices. We do not proselytize. (Juraci)

"Well interesting and fairer. (Observed the seer)

"It's our way of seeing the world. (Juraci)

"Could you give us a summary of the vision of connection with the spiritual world? (Messiah)

"Yes, we'll talk about this specifically later. We believe in the existence of evil spirits such as the curupira. Mediation with this occurs through the shamans. In relation to tribes without spiritual guides, communication with the other world occurs in animals, dreams and prophecies. Sometimes drinks are used to bridge the visible and invisible world. (Juraci)

"In the white world, the link to the other world is through the spiritual heads of every religion and medium. (Messiah)

"The names change, but the function is the same. (Concludes Juraci)

"It's true my friend. (Messiah)

"Do you like parties? (Emanuel)

"Much. We celebrate the important events being the best known of them, the Kuarup, ritual that honors the dead where we exchange gifts, share meals and experiences. There are also games, dancing and singing. (Juraci)

"I love too. Like any young person of my age, getting out is always fun. (Emanuel)

"Indigenous leadership. (Affirmed Juraci)

"Is it true that the first Indians were naked? (The Seer)

"Sometimes our race has always preserved naivety and purity, and so nakedness did not cause shame. On occasion of feasting and ceremony, feathers or fibers were used. Some tribes used slap sex, penis protectors and fabric thongs. Nowadays we already have acculturated Indians and dress according to common standards (Juraci)

"How is the body cleanliness? (Messiah)

"We are very vain and careful with the body. We practice the art of daily bathing. At this the white copied us. (Juraci says proudly)

"How nice. (Messias)

"How was the question of virginity? (Emanuel)

"It's of no value to us, we're sexually active even before we get married. (Juraci)

"Very good. (Emanuel)

"What other aspects of sexuality can you emphasize? (The Seer)

"The prepubescent, the women in the menstruation and the puerperium are interposed for sex. Some accept group sex, incest, adultery, and homosexuality. In the past, one did not have the awareness of shame, sex and hygiene were practiced in the sight of anyone. (Juraci)

"Intense. Their behaviors are really different from ours. (The son of God)

"Each of our features make up our personality. (Juraci)

"What other important features can you mention? (Messias)

"Who practice witchcraft against a member of the tribe is executed; his sons and his wife reject a cowardly man; in a prison, there was no need for confinement, for to flee is dishonor; women cannot desecrate the house of men; the crimes did not prescribe. (Juraci)

"Fair. (Messias)

"How is the relationship between you, the land and the environment in general? (Emanuel)

"The earth is our mother; we depend on her for everything. Animals, plants for us are regarded as Gods offering themselves ceremonies. Creation is a divine work, life itself is interrelated, and the planet is considered sacred. We practice sustainable development so that we do not harm the environment. We do it in this way so that it perpetuates and can feed future generations. This is a lesson to be learned by you. (Juraci)

"An extremely important lesson. (Agreed Emanuel)

"How do you deal with modernity? (The Seer)

"The white man is responsible for the degradation of the planet's natural resources. Many animals important to our survival are simply disappearing. Even among us Indians, reality has changed. Commercial craftsmanship is already a reality between us representing an important source of income. (Juraci)

"Increasingly modern times that really change everyone's life. The important thing is to try to keep the traditions. (The son of God)

"Yes, it's true. For my part, I will continue to be "Fruit of the Earth". (Juraci)

"In your opinion, what is the greatest heritage of your people and what is the current situation? (Messias)

"The greatest heritage of a people is education and understood in education is the language. We do not have a known writing system so teaching-learning occurs on the basis of orality. Before the arrival of Cabral to Brazil there were about one thousand three hundred spoken native languages. Today, it is estimated that two hundred and seventy-four remained. Some of these are almost extinct due to the small number of speakers. If we take into account only those that have been studied in depth, this number is reduced to only nine percent. They are divided into two large linguistic trunks, the tupi and the macro-jê. Within this larger division, there are dialects and variations.

"A very important inheritance. (Messias)

"What replaced the writing system in your culture? (Emanuel)

"Some groups developed a system of signals and other graphs bearing specific meanings that were transmitted from generation to generation. Alongside animal figures, these symbologist reconstitute a historical past so that we can understand a little of our ancestors. It is our legacy to the world. What a pity that this wealth has been lost over time based on the advance of civilization with its premeditated vandalism. (Juraci)

Tears trickle down Juraci's face and our friends come to him trying to calm him down. It was a pity that our origins were lost because of the irrationality of certain people who did not value their own culture. When he recovers, the conversation can then be restarted.

"Could you give us details about this culture? (The Seer)

"Our culture is phenomenal. We have great diversity of accoutrements and objects decorated; we organize wonderful rituals. Our painting is lively and generous, we are simple, we like music and we develop several rhythms, we have a sophisticated oral tradition and our language is very rich. We also have special predilection for dance, handicrafts and feather art. (Juraci)

"Very good. (The Seer)

"There were specific people who produced the art? (Messiah)

"No. Everyone in the village had skill. In our view, the production of symbolic objects of culture was under the influence of spirituality, including the raw materials used in its making. Examples of this, the red feathers are seats of protective spirits used in order to ward off evil. The tincture of arumã is sacred because its constitution is compared to that of the human being. The Kayapó carving symbolizes the village itself. There are geometric patterns in our handicrafts, marks of each tribe. (Juraci)

"Got it. (Messiah)

"What is the importance of music? (Emanuel)

"It's very important. Seen as divine, it is received through dreams. For us, the sound is magical, having great importance in the constitution of the cosmos and in cures. It does not dissociate from the sacred. The songs show traditional stories of our people. There is no mysticism without music. We also celebrate love and nostalgia in music. (Juraci)

"Interesting. Listening to music distracts me and excites me. For me it is also sacred. (Emanuel)

"One more of our inheritance. (Juraci)

"What was the first contribution of indigenous identity to Portuguese culture? (The Seer)

"Once we got here, we taught the whites survival techniques in the jungle in relation to dangerous situations and guidance. In all the projects deployed on this earth, we were serving as guides and servants. Throughout the colonization, we have been present on important occasions such as wars and acting as labor on the fronts of agricultural and extractive expansion. (Juraci)

"Name other important contributions. (Requested Messiah)

"In the Portuguese language, enriching it with several words: Iguaçu, Manaus, Ubiratam, Xavante, etc. In culinary knowledge such as the products derived from cassava and the knowledge in traditional medicine coming to dominate about two hundred thousand species of medicinal plants. There are many possibilities for solutions to many of humanity's present ills. Biopiracy is the greatest enemy with many men of bad faith usurping the collective intellectual property rights of indigenous people. The indigenous population is the main defender of our natural resources. (Juraci)

"Very good. (Messias)

"It's all for today. We have to take care of our chores and get ready for the night that promises to be long. (Juraci)

"That's right. (Messias)

"It's ok. (The Seer)

"What is the next step? (Emanuel)

"Find food for dinner. Are you willing? (Juraci)

"Yes. (The others)

"So, let's go. (Juraci)

The order of the expedition chief is heeded. The four of them leave for a walk around the tent. Choosing a less complicated trail, our friends begin to tread the path for survival. It was already a bit late and they would have a short-term goal to reach today's goals. The weather was good, the sky blue, birds screamed in stampede back to the treetops and with it all conspired for the success of the venture. What awaited them in the future? What would it be like to sleep on a land that is sacred to local residents? Certainly, they would have great surprises and it was personally an honor to have the opportunity to experience an experience similar to the one on the mountain. The change referred to the characters who were different except for the author of the story itself.

After completing five hundred meters of course, with the guidance of the host, they arrive in an orchard and planted culture. They collect guava, banana, coconut and cassava. From there they walk a few meters and find a lake. Demonstrating an incredible ability, the host fishes some fish. Ready. The feast of the first night was complete. As soon as they finish, they start the course of the course back.

The trio of the children of the light is satisfied with the results. They convinced themselves that this had been the best choice, to live with a savage and acculturated sage was truly formidable. Juraci reunited the two opposing forces and presented himself as a link between the past and the present of his people. Getting in touch with this was a great gift that others should enjoy to enjoy.

It was in an environment of stillness and peace that they complete the journey. When they arrive, they light a fire and using the available utensils, they begin to cook the fish. The preparation is by the seer, a master in cooking. Others wait patiently.

When the fish are ready, they divide them equally among themselves in a great communion ritual. Among them, there was no selfishness or dispute, they were brother-children of the same spiritual father. They were truly "fruits of the earth." Afterwards, they finish eating the fruit.

Night fell all over the forest. The cold and the darkness descend into the earth. Our friends are standing by the fire to keep warm. Inevitably, a conversation begins between them.

"I propose an exercise between us. I have already taught a good part of my wisdom to you, now it is your turn to share some of your lives. Comment on the observations related to the moment in which we are living. (Asked Juraci)

"This moment is being crucial to my life. The reunion with my old friend of war has rekindled some marks of my past that are painful. At the same time, it rescued my self-esteem making me feel useful. I know that at the end of this adventure we will not be the same. (Said Messiah)

"I feel the same, my friend. This moment is an important milestone in our lives. (Juraci)

"Come here was a pleasant surprise. I did not know my father's past, nor was I aware of the importance of the indigenous ethnicities to my people. Breaking, I'm once again by my biggest idol. (Emanuel)

"Thank you, my fellow adventurer. Being here with you on another adventure in my series is precious. I hope to contribute a bit more to literature, aiming the well-being of readers and learning the secret of the earth. I am hoping to accomplish myself professionally and spiritually. (The son of God)

"It sure is enriching for all of us. Everyone here deserves happiness, success and greater good. We must do our part so that the spirits of good can act and bless us. We may not have everything we pursue, but we certainly will have what we deserve. (Juraci)

"I believe. (The Seer)

"With whom did you learn to have so much faith? (Inquired Messiah)

"Life and my father taught me. There were so many failures, disappointments, rejections, fits that I learned and grew. With the blessing of my father, I am a transformed man today. (The son of God)

"Very well. It's good to see you happy. Our future will be glorious. (Messias)

"Amen. (Divine)

"This is our son of God, a nice guy, optimistic, generous, charitable and above all human. Since I met you, I have a deep admiration for your work and I am proud to be a part of this series. (Emanuel)

"Thanks for the compliment. Without you, I am nothing, too. (Aldivan)

Tears of emotion trickle down the face of the little dreamer before the memories of the past. Your adventure friends come together and together give each other a hug. It was all that our idol needed to feel comfortable, happy and fulfilled. It was a new era of strength, prosperity and success that he had to manage. At least now, he had prospects.

When it gets calmer, the small meeting is undone and they continue to enjoy the evening among more conversations, observation of the starry sky and reflection. Without realizing it, time passes and they feel the fatigue due to the effort of the bodies during the day. By common consent, they decide to sleep. The next day would bring more news.

Hypotheses of origin of the indigenous people

A new day comes. Birds sing, the cool breeze of morning invades the hut's environment and the sun rises vigorously on the horizon. Soon our friends wake up and try to do their morning activities. They raise, prepare the breakfast, and serve themselves and, at the end of these stages, they begin the debates concerning the next challenge whose main sections are described below:

"Where did the human race come from? (Emanuel)

"We are descendants of Homo Sapiens that originated in Africa some two hundred thousand years ago. From there, the first migratory currents left initially for the Middle East spreading by Europe and Asia. The populations were isolated and adapted to the respective environments developing their own characteristics. (Explained Juraci)

"Super interesting. (Emanuel)

"Specifically, what is the origin of the American people? (Messias)

"The Amerindians are descendants of the group that populated Asia. Probably, the passage was made by the Bering Strait during the ice age. The temperature drops formed blocks of ice by lowering the sea level and exposing the earth by creating this connection. From this point, the population moved to the center and south of America. (Juraci)

"Pure experience. (Messias)

"What are the oldest people in the Americas? (The Seer)

"No one knows for sure. Admittedly, we have the peoples of Clovis who lived in New Mexico-United States whose records pointed to fifteen thousand years ago. However, there are indications that there are even older civilizations. (Juraci)

"Got it. (The Seer)

The colonization

"How did the native population live before the arrival of the Portuguese? (Emanuel)

"Insulated by the Andes Mountains, they maintained retrograde practices practically still living in the prehistory ignoring common technologies like the wheel, the mirror and the firearms. Therefore, the arrival of the Portuguese was a shock for us. (Juraci)

"What happened soon after the start of colonization? (Messias)

"He started the process of acculturation. European culture was soon imposed because of its superiority. To the stranger, we were only pieces that were delivered to his greed. This mentality has provided one of the greatest ethnic massacres in the history of mankind. (Juraci)

"What was the role of religious groups in this era? (The Seer)

"They participated actively in the colonization process. The missionaries acted as evangelizers, peacemakers, teachers, physicians, and artists in general, meeting the needs of the local people. Villages were formed administered by parish priests where the Indians were protected from barbarism. The sad part is that much of our cultural roots have been lost in this process. (Juraci)

"It's really a shame. (The Seer)

"Truth. (Juraci)

"What were the benefits of colonization for the indigenous population? (Emanuel)

"No doubt about it was the technology. Many natives left their villages and went to live by white. Examples of benefits were: the hook that facilitated fishing; the use of the metal ax reduced the work of cutting things; the introduction of species such as banana, jackfruit, mango and orange offered food variety for the tribe; the introduction of horse and cattle facilitated transportation; the plowing of the land in the crops; the domestication of the dog among others. (Juraci)

"What was basically the romantic chain known as Indianism? (Messias)

"It occurred in the nineteenth century. The Indian came to be called "Good savage." Derived from the Enlightenment, the Indian was regarded as the owner of a good moral being a victim of the process of acculturation. This conception was adopted by the government and implemented a broad reform in almost all sectors. On our side, however, the situation was quite different. The white society did not accept us as equals while remaining the process of slavery. The result is that the population has been reduced from five million to just six hundred thousand. (Juraci)

" What other reasons for such a precipitous drop in population? (Messias)

"In addition to slavery, wars and persecutions the great mortality was due to the contagion of diseases brought by the Europeans against whom the Indians had no immunity because they had lived long isolated. (Juraci)

"Sad. (Messias)

"What happened to this surviving population? (The son of God)

"Great part was acculturated and over the years is no longer considered indigenous. (Juraci)

"Lasting a small number currently preserving traditions as an example this tribe. (Aldivan)

"Exactly my dear. (Juraci)

Indigenous education

"What do you mean by indigenous education? (Emanuel)

"He means the process of transmission and production of indigenous knowledge, while school education encompasses indigenous and non-indigenous knowledge. It is a necessary institution to insert the individual in the context of society. (Juraci)

"What conception do you have about education? (Messias)

"First there was resistance on our part because we believed that school education was an exclusive means of acculturation. This concept has changed over time and today we believe that education is a fundamental process of strengthening indigenous identity and culture. (Juraci)

"Modern times. (Observed Messiah)

"Everything changes. (Juraci)

"How is the pedagogical practice practiced in the villages? (The Seer)

"It integrates the elements related to each other: Territory, language, economy and kinship. The most complicated ones to work on are territory and language. (Juraci)

"What are pedagogical cycles and what phases do they mark? (The Seer)

"In our culture cycles are steps that mark the various stages of life. The main ones are: Life before birth: It is considered a blessing the announcement of a pregnancy and is celebrated with commitments established by parents, family and community. The goal is to protect the child and ensure its integral development until adulthood. It should be noted that there is no prejudice among us even if the child is born disabled. We also teach our children the values of charity and generosity. Birth: It is always a sacred time for us, full of rituals and ceremonies. In this stage, the child is blessed by the shaman and is presented to the beings of nature so that no one will harm her. Family education is the responsibility of parents and grandparents. Learning takes place through observation, experimentation and curiosity. Transition from childhood to adulthood: rites of passage represent a kind of graduation. This is the ideal time for young people to demonstrate that they are prepared to assume their responsibility as a member of society. They also need to master the crafts specific to their genre. Among the challenges imposed are survival tests, group of councils and solemn parties. Mature life: It is old age proper and the obligation at this stage is to pass on all the knowledge acquired throughout existence to the children and grandchildren. In our culture, the old are as respected as the young are. (Juraci)

"Extremely exotic. (The Seer)

"What are the main criticisms of indigenous people about the pedagogical processes adopted in their formal schools? (Emanuel)

"The indigenous teaching model reproduces the white school system. Guidelines, objectives, curricula and programs are not appropriate to the context of communities. The teaching material is insufficient; there is no pedagogical supervision. Difficulty in fixing educators in the community due to the absence of decent housing, transportation and food. School feeding is insufficient. Language barrier. (Juraci)

"There is a lot going on. (Emanuel)

"Enough. (Agreed Juraci)

"What is the declaration of principles of the Movement of indigenous teachers of the Amazon? (Messias)

"Serve as a parameter to what we think about school and its goals. Their arguments are: indigenous schools must have specific curricula and regiments developed by the indigenous community. Within the village itself, the direction and supervision of schools should be indicated. Their own culture, art and language should be valued; representatives of the indigenous community should have access to the public agencies responsible for their education. Qualification of teachers. Salary isonomy. Guarantee of continuity in school. Right to integrated health and education. Sufficient equipment for research activities. Use of mother tongue. The school must play a role of territorial defense and biodiversity. The truth about the culture and history of indigenous people in other schools is demanded. Official recognition of education by the Ministry of Education. National school coordination should be ensured with the participation of indigenous teachers. (Juraci)

"Very good. There are many claims but I suppose there are few actions. (Messias)

"Exactly, my dear. (Juraci)

"The indigenous people are famous for having their own teaching-learning environment. What do they currently have? (The Seer)

"We have some specifics. The family and the community are responsible for the education of the children, and this teaching is focused on practical reality: hunting, fishing, agriculture, handicrafts, medicine, nature and other important activities. The knowledge of the chiefs is within the reach of all; we perpetuate good values such as observation, charity, love and cooperation. All are integrated into a teaching-learning process. (Juraci)

"What are the main principles of OIT Convention 107? (Messias)

"Universalization of the right of formal education. Consideration of differentiated socioeconomic reality. The fight against prejudice against indigenous peoples. The official recognition of indigenous languages. (Juraci)

"What is the current reality of indigenous education? (Messias)

"With legal instrumentation through LDB, the government has earmarked large resources for indigenous education both inside and outside reserves, including in higher education. Involving directly the natives, grouped in associations, there is great difficulty in implanting a teaching that preserves the traditions of the ancestors due to the complexity of the subject. (Juraci)

"What is the general objective of indigenous education and what are the difficulties encountered? (The Seer)

"A flexible profile is found adaptable to the needs of the communities, preserving the mother tongue and didactic material prepared by indigenous teachers. The greatest difficulty is the precariousness of educational infrastructures in the villages according to a study by Rangel & Liebgott. (Juraci)

"What sort of needs would these be? (The Seer)

"Lack of facilities and transport, scarce snacks, insufficiency of teachers and didactic materials as already mentioned. Now, I ask a question. How is our culture being spread among whites today? (Juraci)

"Today, the indigenous theme is part of the school curriculum in all undergraduate grades. Many museums, culture points, groups and institutes are dedicated to spreading the wealth and diversity of the archaeological, artistic and historical heritage of its people. (The Seer)

"How nice. I hope they are speaking good about us. (Juraci)

"Certainly. It's the least we can do to minimize an unfair and gloomy past. (The Seer)

"Good. How about we take a break? I'm already a little hungry. (Emanuel)

"Great idea. I'm starving, too. (The Seer)

"What do you think, my friend, Messias? (Juraci)

"I apologize. It's been a long time. (Messias)

"If everyone agrees, who am I to oppose? Let's prepare lunch. Do I count on your help? (Juraci)

"Yes. (The others)

The four musketeers will accomplish the task. With the ingredients left over from the previous day, they begin to prepare the different possible dishes. All cooperate in the works, which demonstrates the great union that existed between them. If they remained in this fighting spirit, nothing would be impossible for the group that had already conquered the whole world through their beautiful adventures. We were in the third stage. The first began a cycle of learning in which they formed as masters of light. In the second, the goal was to help a friend recover from his "Wounded Marks" and at the same time get to know each other a little more. They succeeded in both and were well under way at the present time.

Lunch is ready. Dividing equally between themselves, they begin to feed themselves. This moment was considered sacred for them, prevailing silence, contemplation and reflection. There was much to consider after a few days in the woods in a secluded place. They left everything behind: work, social commitments, family and their own world. There they were like children learning to take their first steps and there was nothing better than knowing their origins.

When they finish eating, a new meeting is scheduled to begin immediately.

Health

"How was indigenous health before the arrival of the Portuguese? (Emanuel)

"According to reports, the natives had bigger and stronger bodies than the Europeans because they were trained in the military arts, in the production of artifacts, in the construction of huts, in physical activities, in hunting, in fishing, in agriculture, in sports. In the old days, there were Indians who lived until their advanced old age in good health, knowing up to four generations of descendants. (Reported Juraci)

"How was the medicine of that time? (Messias)

"Healing practices were ritual character, possessing religious connotations with diseases being attributed to supernatural powers. In medicine, we used herbs, animal products and invasive procedures such as bleeding and scarification. Health workers were commonly the shaman, prayers, healers, herbalists, and midwives. Diverse knowledge was used by the colonizers and incorporated into the current indigenous health system. (Juraci)

"Tell us in brief the health history of your people. (The Seer)

"As already mentioned, with the arrival of the Portuguese in the Brazilian territory, there were numerous epidemics of disease that decimated whole populations with this problem persisting until now. The organs that are responsible for our health are FUNAI (National Indian Foundation) and FUNASA (National Health Foundation). In 1990, the system was decentralized by creating the indigenous health care subsystem and thirty-four health districts. However, the attendance was always irregular. In 2010, under pressure, the government created a special secretariat to address the issue linked to the Ministry of Health. There are also the Indigenous Health Councils that count on the participation of community members. Even with all this equipment, the deficiencies persist. (Juraci)

"What are the common epidemics among the natives? (Emanuel)

"Anemia, diarrhea, tuberculosis, skin diseases, respiratory infections, obesity, hypertension, diabetes mellitus and malnutrition. The lack of coverage and the low-resolution capacity of the services available predominate. (Reported Juraci)

"What are the biggest difficulties you find in terms of health? (Messias)

"The problems occur due to the multiple cultural realities preventing a single health policy, the lack of technical preparation, the great distances and the difficult access to the villages, the precarious infrastructure and the lack of funds. (Juraci)

"What progress have been reached lately? (The Seer)

"The large population growth, the training of many indigenous health professionals and a significant reduction in child mortality. (Juraci)

"What is the indigenous concept for diseases? (Emanuel)

"For us, there is no natural, hereditary, or biological disease. It is always deserved morally or spiritually. There are two ways to get diseases: Triggered by people (Jobs done) or caused by nature (Reaction to an act of yours). (Juraci)

"Very interesting. And what would these actions be like? (Emanuel)

"Man, as well as the spirits that surround him have one good side and one evil side. When there is a conflict between these two forces, it is at the moment that the disease originates. (Juraci)

"Amazing. I have never heard of it. (Emanuel)

"It is a new worldview. It is good to be here. (The Seer)

"It has been an honor, friends. (Juraci)

"What would your concept of nature be? (Messias)

"Nature is also dual, composed of natural and spiritual beings forming a whole. All things have soul from a simple plant, stone or even the human being. (Juraci)

"What is the main health agent in a tribe? (Emanuel)

"In this role is the shaman, a wise man who knows the secrets of nature. (Juraci)

"What is the specific role of the shaman? (Emanuel)

"He has the function of managing and maintaining the natural balance of things, ensuring the survival of all. It has the power to heal or even cause illness and death with the aim of restoring the natural balance. It is also a protector of nature. (Juraci)

"Nice. Got it. Very cool. (Emanuel)

"tell some of your people's health-related beliefs. (The Seer asked)

"You cannot eat raw meat as this can cause stomach diseases. After getting in touch with nature, you cannot eat anything without first taking a shower because it can cause fever, headaches or toothache. Menstruated women cannot go to the woods or the river because they are vulnerable to spiritual attacks, causing the madness or birth of handicapped children. (Juraci)

"Very good. (The Seer)

State policies applied to natives

"Tell us a little about the arrival of the Portuguese and the consequences of this fact. (The Seer)

"As soon as they arrived, the whites began a gradual process of reorganizing our lands. The advance of colonization meant a mass extinction of our peoples due to wars, transmitted diseases and acculturation. This process began on the coast and gradually reached the interior. (Explained Juraci)

"What is the current indigenous population and how is it distributed? (Messiah)

"According to the 2010 census of IBGE (Brazilian Institute of Geography and Statistics) we are 896,900 Indians distributed in 688 reserves and some urban areas. We also have thirty-two groups not yet contacted according to FUNAI. (Juraci)

"What is the mark that allowed highlighting the indigenous issue? ((Emanuel)

"It was the process of democratization during the eighties that encouraged the broad discussion of our question and the action of our own community. (Juraci)

"But, when reality began to change? (Emanuel)

"With the promulgation of the 1988 constituent, there has been a change in the conceptual and legal paradigm of Indian politics. The autonomy and specific rights of our people were guaranteed. It also guaranteed our right to enjoy our traditional lands. There was also decree n.7056/09 which restructured the indigenes bodies. (Juraci)

"What is the latest phenomenon between you? (The Seer)

"An intense deconcentrating of actions, which presupposes a sharing of responsibilities between the involved organs. (Juraci)

"How is this phenomenon developing? (The Seer)

"It was not widely incorporated so that FUNAI is often called upon to express itself whose object is not the responsibility of the autarky. (Juraci)

"How do you find the cooperation between the organs? (Messias)

"We have several examples of cooperation between FUNAI and the other bodies although in terms of actual results it is only a palliative measure because it involves political interest. (Juraci)

"What suggestion would you give to improve this reality? (Emanuel)

"The creation of a national system that would allow a greater integration of the general objectives of my people. (Juraci)

"What are the concepts of protection and promotion regarding the indigenous issue? (Messiah)

"The concept of protection ensures the rights of indigenous non-infringement and the concept of promotion breaks with the welfare history and patronage of public policy. (Juraci)

"How is the question of violence between you? (Emanuel)

"The crime rate has skyrocketed due to the easy access to the indigenous areas, the increase of road and waterway networks, the investment in infrastructure in the country and especially because of insufficient actions of social promotion, territorial protection and articulated security.

"How is the process of demarcation of your lands? (Messias)

"As already mentioned, after the promulgation of the 1988 constituent an obligation was imposed on the state to demarcate and protect indigenous lands. (Juraci)

"What progress has been made in protecting isolated indigenous peoples? (The Seer)

"Advances in their location, aiming and making possible their protection beyond the consolidation of their full possession of their respective territories. Establishment of specific public policy programs and inter-ministerial working groups established with the objective of establishing special health policies for them. (Juraci)

"What is the mission of FUNAI (National Indian Foundation) and what are the biggest difficulties faced by the agency? (The Seer)

"Coordinate the process of formulation and implementation of the indigenist policy of the Brazilian state, establishing effective mechanisms of social control and participative management aiming at the protection and promotion of indigenous peoples. In relation to the difficulties, the main ones are: Personnel deficit and insufficient resources (Juraci)

"Nice. Very good. (Aldivan)

The Indians today

" Tell us a bit about the process of acculturation. (Requested Messiah)

"Since the arrival of the Portuguese, our relationship has been very problematic. With the beginning of colonization, the process of acculturation was inevitable and with that, we lost much of our identity. The law of the strong prevailed. (Lamented Juraci)

"What is the real reflection of this process? (Messias)

"The conflicts over land that have resulted in the expulsion of many indigenous peoples from their lands, the loss of traditions and culture beyond the mass destruction of the population due to diseases, poverty, drugs, prostitution and violence. (Juraci)

"Do you mean that this situation lasts since colonization? (Emanuel)

"Exactly. It was a systematic genocide. (Juraci)

"What is your biggest claim now? (The Seer)

"The possession of our lands. Because of the serious conflicts, we are often forced to abandon them and live-in cities and face an even worse situation of survival. (Juraci)

"Has anything positive been revealed in the last few years? (The Seer)

"Our political awareness has grown; we have support from various organs and we are mobilized through associations such as the "Articulation of the indigenous peoples of Brazil" that represents us nationally. (Juraci)

"Tell us aspects of the internal articulation of your people. (Messias)

"The first indigenous associations emerged from the seventies due to a process of awareness of the tribes organized by the Catholic Church. The debate on the 1988 constitution strengthened the process and a powerful nationwide integration through the Articulation of the Indigenous Peoples of Brazil (APIB) has recently been achieved. (Juraci)

"With the passage of time, did indigenous miscegenation occur with other races? (Emanuel)

"Yes, but this process was not as intense as the miscegenation between the Portuguese and the Africans. According to data from FUNAI (National Indian Foundation), twenty-five percent of the Amazonian indigenous population already lives in cities and only half are considered indigenous. Already the indigenous ascendants are several million. (Juraci)

"Are these ascendants technically indigenous? (Emanuel)

"No. Authentic Indians have declined greatly since colonization. It is estimated that at the time of the discovery in Brazil they had a thousand people and five million people. In the sixties, there were only a hundred and twenty thousand. The government then acted and through aid programs managed to make that population grow again. According to data from the 2010 census, the indigenous population is 817,963 individuals (Juraci)

"What is ethno-genesis? (The Seer)

"It is a process in which mixed groups require the status of indigenous people. It is a process of social and political background that is based on self-identification. For some, they do not deserve the same treatment of the pure Indians and at the same time, they are not civilized at a great risk of losing their rights. (Juraci)

"What is the current state of demarcation of indigenous reserves? (Messias)

"With the creation in 1961 of the indigenous parks of the Xingu (The first Brazilian indigenous reserve) gave the fuel necessary for other peoples also to fight for their self-determination and right to land. Recently, through the National Policy of Environmental and Territorial Management of Indigenous Lands, it is possible to have good perspectives in this sense. (Juraci)

"What is the model of land assignment practiced in Brazil? (Messias)

"In the Brazilian model, the reserves are inalienable assets of the Union ceded for possession and usufruct for life of us, indigenous. (Juraci)

"What message would you give the white man regarding the fulfillment of your claims? (Emanuel)

"The primary condition for a good relationship between us is the guarantee of our land. There is no other way but to guarantee our access to life, culture and a dignified existence. (Juraci)

"What are the consequences of the intense conflicts related to land ownership? (The Seer)

"The destruction of our roots. With the advancement of acculturation and pressure, are already a few tribes that live according to their old practices. Due to the poor living conditions, indigenous migration to the cities occurs. (Juraci)

"How does current development affect the indigenous people? (Messias)

"With the exploitation of our lands, our environment is destroyed and polluted. Examples are mining projects, hydroelectric power plants, logging, agriculture, land grabbing and infrastructure works. Not to mention that we did not earn virtually any compensation on that. (Juraci)

"What other difficulties do you have? (Messias)

"The productive models adopted by us complicate the establishment of effective policies. We have no formal institutions for the production and distribution of products. Nor do we have the technological apparatus of whites. Usually, our economy is subsistence. (Juraci)

"What are the criteria of self-definition most accepted by your people?

"Respect to the traditions; earth love; defined rules; defined language, culture and religion; identify yourself as an Indian and bind yourself to your people. (Juraci)

A stop is promoted and it is decided by consensus to close the day's work. They would save their strength for the next day with assimilation of new knowledge. So far, the white man's contact with one of the remaining natives had been very enriching. Their culture was vast and important.

The afternoon was already falling and they busy themselves with some work. They go to get food in the woods and when they get it, they return to the cabin to prepare dinner. The moment is of great deconcentrating in the group with the empathy increasing between them. Was there anything possible for those dreamers? Probably not because they have already demonstrated in the adventures of once they were capable. They were fighters, warriors and above all believers. Together, they formed a fantastic quartet destined to conquer the world. They deserved it.

When the dinner is ready, they distribute among themselves the available food: Chicken baked with cornstarch. It was delicious and they take the break from the food to exchange important information. Nothing could go wrong for his pretensions.

Confident, happy, willing and accomplished our four musketeers were aware of their role in the contribution of Brazilian culture. Each of them owned an unequaled culture that was to be passed on to the common good. They were the part of the group "Sons of Light" and thus they had their own identity.

After dinner, they enjoy the rest of the evening around the campfire telling each other their personal life.

"I feel very fortunate in my personal and professional life. It is true that I have not yet achieved everything, but my attitude of life shows how great man I am. I can define my life in three important moments: Childhood, The dark night of the soul and the current phase. My childhood was marked by oppression and family love, doubts, seclusion, misery, disbelief, prejudice, fear and lack of action. Being a boy was very good and at the same time, a great challenge. Full of impossible dreams, I grew up in the habit of reading, sustaining myself day after day. Without conditions at that time, it was all a mere desire. I became a teenager and I started facing the harsh reality of a developing country. When I finished my studies, I did not get a job placement and then there was depression and then a period of darkness. All left me leaving only my family, my spiritual father and my angel. That's why I make it a point to say that the family, however bad it may be, is an important part of my life because it is always present in the good and bad times. I seriously injured the nerves at this stage of my life, which brought more complications. With that, a part of me died and I was never the same again. But what did I have to complain about? I was alive and much better than other people. When you get to the bottom of the well, you need to have a critical eye and see that this well is not that deep. There are those suffering from incurable diseases, there are the orphans, children on the street, there are those without love, there are those without hope and there are the evil ones who do not have the privilege of loving. I always loved and believed even in the clutches of darkness. The point of ransom was when my angel prevented me from returning to a certain spiritual center. From then on, I promised to change and in return my God supported me constantly. I overcame my dark night; I went back to school and I got a job. At the current stage. I became an adult and resumed writing. Despite being a stranger, I am sure that I am fulfilling my role for the spread of culture in a country as needy as ours. (The Seer)

"I was born in the Xukuru tribe and from an early age, I learned from my parents the value of my culture and the value of the land itself. I recognized myself as a fruit of the earth at all times. By dissenting politics, I was exiled from the conviviality of my people and I had to work hard on a farm in Ibimirim. I remember well the painful tasks, the whip, the privations, and the uncertainty of tomorrow. What was good about this time was friends. Among them, the dear Messias. Afterward, I received the amnesty from the head of my people and then returned to my land. It had been years, and with a new vision, I was no longer the same. My goal was to use my knowledge of the white man to try to preserve my culture. Time was passing and with it I got new experiences. Today, I am what I am and I am very proud. I am an accomplished man. (Juraci)

"I came as a baby from Italy and as soon as I understood, I loved this land. We arrived in São Paulo to work on the coffee farms. Due to serious misunderstandings, we moved to the northeast and here I went to work on a farm. In it, I met my great friend Juraci. Suffering strengthened our friendship and we spent beautiful moments together. After separation, we had little contact, but the feeling did not change. I grew up, I had a beautiful son and I became a master of light. Looking at everything that has passed, I see myself the same way. The difference is that I'm more experienced. (Messias)

"My family is of Italian origin but I was born in a Brazilian crib. I learned from my father the good values a man must have. Despite the great difficulties we face over time, we are happy. My greatest achievement was to have saved the life of the child of God when he needed it most. It was a blessing to meet him and to be participating in this important literary series. (Emanuel)

"Very good. Our personal stories reveal a little of our personality. The important thing is to be aware of what was experienced, to forget the hurts and pains trying to be happy. (The Seer)

"Yes. Our goal is this. (Juraci)

"What is the next step? (The Seer)

"Try to sleep after a day full of debates. There is still much to consider about the traditions of my people. (Juraci)

"Yes. (The Seer)

"Very good. I am sleepy. (Messias)

"Me too. (Emanuel)

"So, let's go. (Juraci)

Juraci's request sounded like an order and they all retreating to the hard, dry ground of the hut. It was not comfortable, but they were already accustomed. Life in the jungle was a great adventure because of the distance of the family, the abandonment, the difficulty of feeding and the natural dangers. This enriched the story that was already in its third chapter. In the first, the voices of light, is the first book in the children of light series whose main theme is the religious and relationships between people. It aims to inform, reflect, question values and put us before historical facts. The second title, Bruised Wounds, shows that we all carry important marks of pain and discouragement in the face of life's events. What to do with this is what many people ask themselves. Bruised Wounds comes to bring a script and at the same time answers to his most disturbing inquiries. It is a highly recommended book for those who have not yet found the path to happiness. These serial adventures made the readers happy.

Remained now for our characters try to sleep.

Indian movement

The morning and night usually went by with our adventurous friends having comforting dreams. The sun rose ripping the horizon with its rays penetrating through the gaps of the humble hut. The natural clarity of the morning helps them to wake up. Almost simultaneously, they rise and begin their journey of responsibility. It really took a great strength of will and detachment so that they could dream of achieving their goals. Among them, the greatest at the moment was to unravel the indigenous culture and pass this knowledge on to the general public. They hoped to succeed.

They begin to prepare breakfast with the ingredients they had on availability. The exercise brings them closer together, creating a stronger bond of empathy between them. How beautiful was that union that had everything to give beautiful fruits? With a little effort, soon the food is ready and they begin to serve themselves.

The moment of the meal is a moment of brotherhood and exchange among the members of that group. They take time to reflect more on the latest events and exchange important information on the next stages of the adventure. Everything was going very well.

Finished the coffee, they meet there and restart the conversation the day before.

"What was an important factor for the ethnic genocide imposed on the indigenous people? (Emanuel)

"It was precisely the ability of the settlers to use the disagreements between the groups to promote internal wars. (Juraci)

"What current situation of coexistence between you? (Messias)

"We have overcome our rivalries and come together for our rights. Since the 1970s, representative organizations have been created. The articulation between these organs forms what we call an organized indigenous movement. (Juraci)

"What is indigenous movement? (The Seer)

"It is the set of strategies and actions that our organizations plan and execute in defense of collective interests. This concept is different from organization because it is not necessary that we participate in a representative entity so that we can act in the indigenous movement. (Explained Juraci)

"What were the first fruits of the work of your representative entities? (The Seer)

"They succeeded in persuading the society and the national constituent congress to approve our advanced rights in the present federal constitution in 1988. There were important advances in land demarcation and regularization. It reached the development of the idea of an indigenous school education that allows us a differentiated teaching and aimed at the preservation of our traditions. Another achievement was the implantation of the indigenous health districts. (Juraci)

"How is the organizational model of your people? (Messias)

"We take the white man's model and its technologies so we can fight for our rights. This does not mean that we leave our essence aside. I continue to be "Fruit of the Earth" capable of resisting, surviving and evolving more and more to preserve the traditions of my people. (Juraci)

"What is indigenous organization? (Emanuel)

"It's the way an indigenous people organize their jobs, their struggle, and their collective lives. The common representatives of these organizations are the cacique, the tuxaua, the leader, the shaman, the teacher, the health agent and the father of the family among others. (Juraci)

"What are the existing types of organization and their characteristics? (Emanuel)

"There are two types of organization: traditional and formal. The traditional organization is the original organization, taking the example of the village. They follow guidelines and rules of operation, relations and social control from the traditions of each people. These organizations are dynamic, multiple, decentralized, transparent, agile and flexible. Decisions are joint or agreed. This type of entity fully meets the internal demands of the community. High-ranking tribe posts are usually inherited from father to son. This is a cosmological orientation constituted since the creation of the world which guides the social, political, economic and spiritual life of individuals and groups. A characteristic of the traditional society that can be highlighted is the social distribution of positions, functions, roles, tasks and responsibility among the members of the group. Among the main subgroups are the specialists in the training of shamans, warriors, hunters, fishermen, utensils and handicrafts. Another peculiarity is the absence of authoritarian power. The formal organization has a legal and formal character. It is a model with social status, general assemblies, board, bank account and accountable to the state. These characteristics make this type of entity institutionalized, centralized, bureaucratized and personalized. The formal recognition of the state is required to enable its functioning. An example of this is the associations that aim to defend the territory and other public policies. (Juraci)

"What are the leadership aspects in the current terms of the indigenous people? (The Seer)

"Before, there were only the traditional leaders, that is, the caciques that represented the community before other peoples. With the emergence of the indigenous organizations, there was a change in this pattern. New people have come to play important roles in the collective life of the tribe, such as association leaders, teachers, health workers, and other professionals. Generally, they represent their people to society in general. There is no selfishness or strife between us, all cohabiting in harmony. (Juraci)

"What is the concept of indigenous association? (The Seer)

"It is a formal entity that aims to organize, mobilize and articulate the struggle of our peoples. There are more than seven hundred organizations distributed in the country attending to the need of the communities. Over time, they have gained importance and assumed other technical activities such as the provision of health services in partnership with the national health foundation. These associations are the result of the political change of the indigenous people and the process of re-democratization of the country. (Juraci)

"What does this type of representation mean to your people? (Messias)

"It is a kind of protector of our people's collective rights to the outside world. At the lowest risk, this entity acts together with village leaders to eliminate the threats. (Juraci)

"Discriminate the history of the contemporary indigenous movement. (Requested Messiah)

"Well, I studied the theory of militant and social scientist Silvio Cavuscens According to it, this history can be divided into periods. The first phase would be governmental tutelary Indianism that lasted approximately a century. Among its main characteristics are the presence of the Indian Protection Service (IPS) later reformulated to become the National Indian Foundation. The IPS was created in 1910 inspired by the European model, which valued man and nature. Even so, there was still the idea that the Indian was an incapable being, which is why he should be under the protection of the state. Following this misguided vision, the IPS came to represent my people inside and outside the country. Parallel to this was an ongoing state action whose goal was the complete assimilation and cultural integration of our peoples with practical significance for the effective appropriation of our lands and denial of our traditions. This absurd idea preached that we should live as whites residing in cities or towns ceasing to be ourselves in order to allow national development. The IPS's job was to provide our minimum needs, which consisted of health, land, education, and subsistence, always with the view that we were incapable. The result of this was the advance in territorial invasions already consummated and opening of new frontiers of expansion. Some strategies were aimed at the complete extinction of our people. Among the main ones, we can mention the attempt to define Indian criteria in order to establish who was Indian. According to this criterion, we were classified as aloof, isolated, non-acculturated in acculturation routes, acculturated and integrated Brazilians. Blood tests were carried out to ascertain our degree of integration. All this to annul our rights and destroy the heritage of our ancestors. The second period is called the non-governmental indigenous one that began in the seventies. Two new actors were introduced: The renewed Catholic Church and the organizations linked to the progressive sectors of the Universities. The Catholic Church created an indigenous pastoral ministry and an indigenous missionary council (IMC). Pastoral care assists us in our basic needs, and IMC has a supportive, articulated, disseminated and denounced role in relation to the violation of our rights. Since then, many other non-governmental organizations (NGOs) have been supporting our cause. It was a period full of mobilizations at local, regional and national level in favor of our rights. This process culminated in the conquests of the 1988 constituent. We realized that with the union we could be much stronger. We also have the third phase called the Indigenist Contemporary Government. During this period, there were several organs operating in our communities, ending the hegemony of FUNAI (National Indian Foundation). Examples of this are indigenous health, which became the responsibility of FUNASA (National Health Foundation) and indigenous school education that came under the seal of the Ministry of Education. With this, the articulation between my people and the government was expanded. We have also diversified our public policies focused specifically on our cause. The most notable fact was the implementation of projects for the indigenous peoples of the Amazon with a wide participation of these. Since then, we have not thought of indigenous politics without our effective monitoring, cooperation and participation, representing a significant advance in the relationship with the state. Regarding the retractions, the state uses its institutions to hamper the implementation of the new indigenes policies and white parliamentarians using their influence have filled the congress of requests that aim to diminish or even annul our rights conquered with so much effort. Convention 169 of the International Labor Organization (ILO) recognizes these rights. This convention rules the social control and our participation in decision-making bodies that refer to our interests. It also recognizes us as Indians, reaffirming our cultural identity in a time of re-democratization of the country. Today, we are respectful for who we are. (Juraci)

"What were the possible causes of the rise of indigenous organizations? (The Seer)

"The need to react to an acculturations policy; proliferation of indigenous non-governmental organizations; decentralization of financial support of public resources and post-war international cooperation; the Federal Constitution of 1988; the retraction of the state; the political-financial emptying of the National Indian Foundation (FUNAI); the globalization of environmental issues and the decentralization of international cooperation. (Juraci)

"How has the indigenous movement been in recent years? (Emanuel)

"In the 1980's, informal, but not very institutionalized, organizations emerged claiming territorial rights and welfare. Through the charismatic leaderships (Young Indian students) together with the Catholic Church and sectors of the academy, they have triggered a remarkable process of mobilizing the tribes in favor of our rights, especially those related to land, our culture and against discrimination and prejudice. In the nineties, our organizations multiplied, assuming functions in the areas of health, education and sustainability. Other discussions have emerged on our agenda as ethno-sustainable discourse. Already in the decade of 2000, the spaces of our representation in the external and internal environment were consolidated, bringing new conquests and challenges. (Juraci)

"What are the main consequences of strengthening the movement of your people? (Messias)

"Our population has grown again. Among the main causes of this are the recognition of indigenous identity (resurgent Indians) and urban Indians as well as greater acceptance by white society. We also had significant territorial achievements. Together, our reserves occupy the 12.38% of the total area of the country. (Juraci)

"What are the big players in the struggle for the rights of their people? (The Seer)

"The relevance of indigenous lands and linguistic and cultural diversity. (Juraci)

"What are the main difficulties faced by your people? (The Seer)

"To deal with the bureaucratic model of the white man's social, political and economic organization; the resistance to the historical seduction of the white world; difficulty of socio-political articulation; reverse the historical process of government dependence, and how to ensure the empowerment of members of indigenous associations. Finally, guarantee our sovereignty and preservation of culture, tradition and values. (Juraci)

Again, a stop is promoted for general rest and task completion. The subject had been exhausted, and they would seek the next few times to address other subjects. They go to the woods and upon returning to the cabin bring more food. They prepare the lunch and when it is ready, they serve themselves. This sacred moment is harnessed intensely in a climate of peace. At the end of the meal, they meet again ready for another round of conversation.

Citizenship, autonomy and indigenous gender

"How is the process of obtaining the citizenship of your people? (The Seer)

"In recent years, through the organized action of our entities, we gradually conquered the status of Brazilian citizen. But what does this mean in practical terms? We have the possibility of enjoying the rights guaranteed to others while we continue to cultivate our values and traditions. However, our goals are far from being guaranteed and respected. Our citizenship is being built with enough difficulties. On the positive side, the term state tutelage was overcome and our leaderships began to gain prominence abroad and abroad. In the negative, the proposed changes were still little implemented. It should be emphasized that citizenship in its broad sense is action and independent union of differences. We have our symbols, values, stories, social systems, political systems, our own legal and economic systems, and that does not make us less important than you. We are also Brazilians. Do not want to overlap your culture and your will like before, because today we live a different reality. Instead of acculturation, there must be respect and preservation of our cultural riches. We are the real Brazilians, while the Portuguese white man is an outsider who came to exploit us and to work out what is ours by right. Enough social injustice and ethnic genocide. We want to get up. We also have to overcome the notion of territorial citizenship because although we do not stop the ownership of our lands, we have the use of its richness as an example of biodiversity and natural resources, which demonstrates our importance in terms of preservation for future generations. Ultimately, citizenship is essential if we are to participate in the world we live in and ensure that our history does not go away. (Juraci)

"What is the effect of technological resources on your routine? (Emanuel)

"Unfortunately, most of the time, the access to technology is used as an exchange to buy our conscience in order to approve interest's contrary to ours. It is worth remembering that despite its importance in today's world, the science and progress do not guarantee the solution of all problems. It must be combined with other social policies so that it has good effects. Among these policies we can mention quality education and health and self-sustainability. Each indigenous people are autonomous to decide the most appropriate use of this and in what perspectives to do so. (Juraci)

"What is autonomy for you and how is it being treated? (Messias)

"Autonomy is everything. We have always been autonomous by defining and organizing activities in the community according to our economic, political, economic, legal and religious vision. We also fight for autonomy in front of the state, overcoming centuries of humiliation, contempt and dependence. In practical terms, it means respect for the development of our cultures, languages, medicines, religiousness, the right to land and the recognition of our organizations. (Juraci)

"What is the indigenous concept of nature and territory? (The Seer)

"Nature and territory are sacred to us. Each component of the environment is important to us as the mountains, lakes, woods, ocean and rivers, rocks, sky, animals and ourselves. The earth is fundamental to our survival and does not dissociate from us. It is not only a material good but the abode of all living things. It is part of our ancestry and our future having relation with the natural and supernatural phenomena. Religion is also very attached to it. We are part of nature and not owners of it and this is a lesson that the white man must learn for life to continue on earth. (Juraci)

"What is gender and how is this reflected in the indigenous world? (Emanuel)

"Gender is the expression of the intervening force of the white world. It reflects the conception that people have of society and of life in general in which each segment is thought of as part of the collectivity even though they are distinct from each other. Mechanism is needed to protect the rights of each group. There is also the individualized right that generates the existence and practice of centralized power in which the collective transfers its power to an individual or group. In this case, the discussion is opened: Would it be legitimate to consider the rights of individuals or of a people in general? Regardless of the answer, the certainty we have is that there is no standard that satisfies all specifications and groups concomitantly. There will always be injustices within the standard of society we know, indigenous or otherwise. Even because the question of values is quite relative between the white man and us. An example of this is that many men leave their old parents in an asylum and think that everything is right. For us this is an aberration and an abandonment. Our society is well organized and structured, we follow cosmological orientations, norms and principles marked by subgroup functions (age groups, clans, shamans, prophets, healers, etc.) that integrated with each other form our ethnic group. All are important, with large or small missions, what matters is the contribution of each to the universe. Genres are so primordial. From the contact with the white man, the tendency is to unconsciously incorporate patterns of relationship. This high pressure makes us increasingly have in our midst so-called modern characteristics. If on the one hand it facilitates our contact with the outside world, it gradually promotes the extinction of our own domain. Reversing this process is our biggest challenge. (Juraci)

Worldview Tupi-Guarani

"We have come to an important part of our trajectory. This is the moment when I will reveal a little of the souls of my ancestors. Are you ready? (Juraci)

"Yes. After everything we have been through, it's the most desired moment. Thank you for your trust. (The Seer)

"I am very anxious. (Emanuel)

"I also want to learn more. (Messias)

"Very good. So, let's begin. Every word, action or object has a spirit. Named, a being has a seat. Spirit is silence, sound and peace. Silence-sound has a rhythm, a melody and a tone. The body is the color. When the spirit is sung, it becomes. Everything that exists intones. Lives happen in succession. The great material and immaterial entities take care of the harmony of the tone. They are the architects of creation directed by the elder deities and Mother Earth itself, who in turn are led by the elder of the race, the earliest ancestors who have become stars. (Juraci)

"Well remembered. I was at the beginning with my father and I am witness of all this. My father and I created the universe by our infinite love for creatures. The land and its inhabitants are but a tiny spot in the immensity that we have created, but they are very important for our project. Among them is my dreams and me. You are right when you say that we should value our origins. We are all stars. (The Seer)

"I understood in this passage the beginning, middle, end and the consistency of things. Analogously to the white myth. (Emanuel)

"Knowing the essence and your beliefs will be a great adventure. (Messias)

"Great observations. Let's continue. The being is named and the spirit awakens. Only the being can understand the mysteries of life that involves the wisdom and knowledge of the ancients. On this path of liberation, we go through rituals, ceremonies, celebrations and initiations that aim at understanding the tradition. The first step starts with the name of things. (Juraci)

"Divine wisdom is given freely to those who seek it. (Divine)

"Traditions are the greatest heritage of a people. (Emanuel)

"The name distinguishes being in the crowd. (Messias)

"We have four great archetypal images of creation: Namandu is our first father; Kuaracy is our mother; Tupā is the unfolding of the whole and the earth is the material world. (Juraci)

"In the Catholic language, we have the Father God, the Son God and the Holy Spirit. (The Seer)

"Kuaracy would be in our tradition the Virgin Mary. (Emanuel)

"Namandu would be Yahweh, Tupan would be Jesus and the earth would symbolize all creatures. (Messias)

"Yes. This would be the most accepted syncretism to represent our Gods. (Juraci)

"A junction of cultures. (The Seer)

"Everything began with the existence of the supreme consciousness that arose by itself having no beginning, middle or end. This being unfolded by creating love and wisdom. (Juraci)

"In our view, Yahweh God is the beginning, middle and end. The father generated Jesus and the Holy Spirit which are love and wisdom respectively. (The Seer)

"Another example of syncretism. (Emanuel)

"The manifesto manifests itself as a space chanting eternal life as wind. The creation of space-time and human languages begins. Language then became the soul. (Juraci)

"The soul is composed by the divine breath, its consciousness and by free will. The melody of the soul are your own choices. (Messias)

"Coordinating this whole process is the hand of Yahweh. (The Seer)

"The creative father consists in mystery and wisdom. Nothing for him is unknown, being attentive to all human activity. (Juraci)

"God father is one manifested in the three divine persons: Father, son and Holy Spirit. He is omnipotent, omniscient, and omnipresent. (Emanuel)

"We still have the mother fire and tupā that come together and correspond. (Juraci)

"Jesus and the spirit are intercommunicated with the father and the will of one of them is the same as the others. (The Seer)

"Tupā presents himself as a hummingbird. Every human being has his hummingbird soul dwelling in the heart of tupā. (Juraci)

"Lord is God. Through his omnipotence and omnipresence, he takes care of everyone's life. (Messias)

"Tupã started the creation of the first land. Five eternal palm trees were created at the four cardinal points and four support columns. (Juraci)

"God created the world in seven days through his word and love. The work of creation never stops. (The Seer)

"The blue palm tree is sacred and symbolizes the dwellings. It represents in the kingdom, the same as the owl and the hummingbird in the animal kingdom. (Juraci)

"Blue is the color of the sky representing all the majesty and sovereignty of Yahweh. From God comes all blessings. (Emanuel)

"Nature repeats macrocosmic dance by guiding us to its rhythm and harmony. There are four corners: Arayama: Original Winter. Arapoty: It's life at its birth. Arakuara-cy-puru: It is the Warmth of life that is realized. Ara pyau ñemokandire: It gives cadence to the time when life falls. These four corners are revealed through the cycles of nature. (Juraci)

"Beautiful wisdom. (The Seer)

"Thank you. (Juraci)

"There were four seasons of cosmic nature. The four directions represent the seasons: north, south, east and west. Each cycle is reflected in trials, challenges and learning for all realms intertwined with all the kingdoms of life (mineral, vegetable, animal, human, supra-human and divine). The symbol is the spider. (Juraci)

"What are these seasons and their characteristics? (Messias)

"The first cycle is ruled by Jakairá, divinity responsible for the spirit, substance, fog and smoke. The land began to be inhabited by the tribes-bird and rainbow people. The bird tribes passed on the sacred mysteries to the coming humanity. The great challenge of this phase was the courage for freedom. Those who did not risk generated fear and, consequently, slavery. The second cycle is of the deity Karai Ru Eté who is the lord of fire and light. The garden was created giving origin to red tribe. The challenge was the discovery of the night and from this point, three spirits were born: The spirit of sleep, the spirit of the dream and the spirit of illusion. In the third cycle, Tupã is the deity, the commander of the seven waters. The great challenge is power. With the evil inheritance of man came the seeds of the past cycles: The soul of fear, sleep, dream, and illusion, enslavement that consequently generated possession, dispute and attachment magnified by greed for power. The fourth stage refers to the tradition of the great mother who is divided into three great traditions: The tradition of the sun, tradition of the moon and tradition of the dream. A synthesis of previous traditions is sought at this stage and it is therefore called the tradition of the great mother in reference to the mother earth that provides for the survival of all. This particular tradition brings together a set of celebrations and teachings handed down from generation to generation. (Juraci)

"What are the foundations of indigenous human language? (The Seer)

"Be, language, soul and word are one. Ayvu is the spirit that is eternal and gives life to the body. The breath of life unfolds in three: ñe'eng, which means soul, ayvu, which is spirit and ñe,'em 'g-cy is the spirit that the thunder deities send to incarnation in the various dimensions. The feminine drives the movement of life with the beginning, middle and end being recreated by the four seasons. The movement of life translates into unconditional love and wisdom. Every person, every mountain. Every tree, every stone, or any other being is important to the balance of the universe. (Juraci)

"Love, truth, faith, claw, and freedom are the same being. He created all visible and invisible elements. I am one of your most important generations because I have the pure soul and the divine essence. My mission is very great: to transmit the teachings of my father so that the whole soul knows it and who knows can regenerate of its great sins. I am not God, but I am his son. I can realize the impossible dreams of people. My name is Aldivan, seer, Divine and son of God. I came to conquer the world at the behest of my father. (Divine)

"I believe. Our traditions believe in the forces of good and since you are this force, I ask for more understanding and judgment for men. (Juraci)

"I always act through good people. Nothing happens on earth without the word not leaving my father's mouth. I can transform the human heart as long as there is a true surrender. I have set you free by my great love. (Fortuneteller)

"I thank you for all, good and bad. I realize that the world will always exist under your wings. Great son of God! (Juraci)

"Yes, as long as the world is a world I will exist forever, my love will never change and my words will not cease. (The son of God)

"So be it. (Juraci)

"Amen. (The others)

"This is the mystery of the human incarnation. A name is a soul-word. Each seed is unique having feminine and masculine aspects. The four elements: earth, water, fire and air generate future seeds whose goal is the perpetuation of life. (Juraci)

"The two components, good and evil, are part of the individual and our attitude in the face of difficulties is what defines our path generating consistent fruits. (The Seer)

"There is also the body that is made of earth wires, fire, air and water intercommunicating in tone levels. We are part of the music of life. (Juraci)

"As well as the melody, that cradles the hearts in love and suffering. (Messias)

"So, we close this cycle. (Juraci)

There is a pause. Our friends return to their normal activities including lunch preparation. All cooperate with each other demonstrating the union of that warrior group, victorious and spectacular. When the food is ready, they serve themselves equally in a climate of peace and harmony. At that moment, all the worries were forgotten and come a good longing from the family and from yesterday. They take advantage of this time to solve doubts, entertain their selves more and rest. At the end of this stage, they meet again to broaden the debate.

The various mythologies

"I'm going to start now with the mythology of the ancients. Are you ready? (Juraci)

"Yes. Must be exciting. (The Seer)

"I've always been very curious. (Emanuel)

"I'd love to discover those secrets. (Messias)

"Very well. So here goes the stories:

Abaangui

At the beginning of time, there were two handsome brothers named Abaangui and Zaguaguayu. Abaangui had two equally clever and handsome children. One day, tired of the monotony of the earth, the two sons of Abaangui threw two arrows toward the sky where they were fixed. After, they threw more arrows that entered the first forming thus chains that united the sky and the earth. Through this link, these children came to the sky where they became the sun and the moon.

Abaçaí

A young Indian from the Xukuru tribe called (name) was very beautiful, polite, respectful and intelligent. She was a sweet girl in dealing with people and decided to keep her virginity unlike Indian custom. Her only fault was to be adventurous, which was the cause of her perdition. One fine day, on a walk in the forest, she was surprised by the spirit of Abaçaí who was in the shape of a lion. Unprotected, the young woman was sexually abused and then lost the soul that had been extracted by the devil. Abaçaí thus made one more victim by sheer imprudence of the girl.

The sign of Andurá

Once, a group of white disliked with our tribe went through the woods around the village setting fire to a criminal fire. Thanks to Tupã, one of our chiefs saw the sign of the Andurá inflamed, a sacred and fantastic tree. A team moved to the place and with much effort managed to put out the fire for the happiness of all. The police who had been warned arrested the criminals. One more example of white malice and the importance of some beings.

Angatupyry and Tau

In the Asian region, we have the concept of Yin and Yang that has spread to the whole world. Yin is the feminine principle, water, passivity, darkness and absorption. The yang is the masculine principle, fire, light and activity.

In our belief, we have the Angatupyr, who is the spirit of good and the Tau who is the spirit of evil. Both guide humanity in what destiny to follow. But with the question of free will the control and the final decision on which course to take is and will always be of man.

The battle between the Carnijó and the Xukuru

In a remote past, there was a disagreement between the Carnijó and Xukuru indigenous groups making them enemies. It was then declared a perpetual war between these peoples. The carnijó were cunning and false and quietly prepared an ambush against our community. At our traditional annual spring festival, our village was attacked on both sides. The battle then began. As we were not prepared, our warriors fell to the ground and the enemy was growing. Already close to being dominated, our shaman began a secret ritual invoking the spirit of Angra, who is the Fire Goddess. She put herself in the battle and with her claw and ferocity was overthrowing our enemies who had no alternative but to escape. Angra is a very powerful spirit. From there, a peace agreement was signed between the peoples and the friendship was resumed. Learn that understanding is better than war. A lesson that life taught me.

A disastrous hunt

From a young age, I learned from my father to hunt and fish. He always told me not to hunt at night because there was a danger that the Anhangá would appear. I never believed this legend until a full moon night hunting a chicken that was trying to escape from my hands appeared the someone. This evil spirit appeared in the form of a deer with eyes of fire, with horns and a cross on his forehead. Speaking in a thunderous voice, he threatened me with death if I did not give up the hunt. I was brave, but in front of this monster, I fainted. I fled from that place leaving everything behind with a speed of a flash and I did not stop until arriving at my village. I did not tell this case to anyone, but I decided to never again hunt at night.

The boitatá

In a distant time, one night advanced in such a way that the day would not exist anymore. The night was very dark, stars, without wind, the weather was dry and without any hiccups. The men were indoors with cold and hunger. They could not go out at night to get firewood or food because of the dangers of the woods. The days passed and a torrential rain began. It was there that a great snake awakened from its deep sleep and began to eat the eyes of the dead animals on the water. Her eyes gleamed and with so many eyes that the snake ate it too, she was all bright. Then she became a brilliant monster known as boitatá.

Boiúna

The boiúna is a giant snake that lives in lakes, rivers or streams. It is often confused with a boat and when the fishermen approach, they see food of her. When this snake grows old, it goes to earth being aided by the centipede in obtaining food.

According to legend, the boiúna impregnated an Indian who gave birth to two twin children being a boy and a girl. The boy was called Honorato and the girl of Maria. The mother wanted to be free of the children and then threw them into the river and there they began to live. Honorato and Maria grew up. While Honorato was good, Maria was very bad causing serious losses. That was when Honorato decided to kill her. It is said that on some moonlit nights, Honorato would leave the charm and become a beautiful boy. There was only one chance of him becoming fully human: It was pouring milk into his snake's mouth and wounding his head until blood ran out. This miracle happened and from there Honorato began to live with his human family and was very happy.

The meeting with the caipora

My father has always advised me about the dangers in the woods, especially about the danger of hunting on Fridays, Sundays, and holy days. However, I was not always listening. I went out on the all the saints day in the woods because I had no food at home. I started touching a deer and the instant I was going to pick it up, the pebble appeared in front of me. He was an Indian with dark skin, agile and naked. The fame of the pebble was not good. Some said he ate the hunters or beat them up and I was not ready for any of the options. Using my wiles, I apologized to this sacred being and to my good fortune, he seemed to conform. At the slightest opportunity I had, I fled and promised never to repeat this feat. The caipora is the protector of the forest animals and is willing to do everything for them.

The legend of Pirarucu

In the beginning of time, there was a wicked, false, smart and greedy Indian named Pirarucu. Their wickedness had no end, causing harm to men and animals. An urgent action was then required of the shaman of his tribe. Through a ritual, tupã was invoked and in answer, he sent a powerful spirit called Chandoré. The envoy from Tupã tried to kill Pirarucu, but it was unsuccessful because he threw himself into the river and became the fish that currently bears his name.

The curupira

The curupira inhabits the Brazilian jungles. He is short, fast, has red hair and his feet are turned back. Headquartered in the darkness of the woods, he loves to rest in a shade of a mango tree. His function is to protect all beings from the forest from the predatory action of man. For this, he uses the whistle or creates terrifying images in order to scare his opponents. In addition, he usually kidnaps children so they can live with him in the woods. So, we are very careful about protecting our children.

Legend of the sun and moon

It all started from the darkness. At a certain moment, by the will of Tupã, the sun was born which we know as Guaraci. Guaraci was delighted with the universe and proud of the light it produced. But one day he had to rest and then everything went dark again. That is where he got an idea. For the world to be enlightened while he slept, he created the moon called Jaci. The created moon was so beautiful that immediately he fell in love. However, when he opened his eyes to contemplate it everything was illuminated and then she disappeared. Guaraci then invented love. Love remained as much in the light as in darkness, being today the greatest force in the universe. Very pleased, Guaraci created the stars to keep his mistress company while he slept. Thus, the universe was expanding.

Lara's spell

This occurred with my grandfather in the late nineteenth century. He was a skillful hunter and fisherman and whenever he could, he made excursions with his friends in the rivers of the region. On one of these occasions, in the region known today as Paulo Afonso-BA, delighting in San Francisco they were victims of a great stratagem of destiny. By the river, they heard a beautiful girl singing and waving at them. They resolved to approach. They were three men who left the boat and went to meet beautiful India. As soon as they came near her, she offered them food and rest from his long journey. They quickly agreed to think there was no harm. She brought fish, juice, rice and angu (corn mixture). She also served everyone with joy, satisfaction and good conversation. Then the time advanced a little and suddenly they felt a little sleep. The girl then suggested that they went to sleep that would guarantee their safety. Until then, no problem. The big surprise was when one of them woke up and witnessed a macabre scene: The young woman was sucking the blood of his other companions who lay without reaction. She was a monster and everything was a frame! Still a little staggering, this person fled back to the boat and immediately returned to earth. By a miracle, he had been saved from the famous Iara, the Goddess of the waters that completed in her curriculum the death of two more victims. My grandfather was one of them unfortunately.

Ipupiara

The case of Ipupiara occurred in 1564 in the captaincy of São Vicente, current state of São Paulo. This was the name given to the supernatural being that appeared there and was killed. The story was as follows: One day almost night, an Indian woman, the slave of a captain, left for a walk. The Indian has gone into the bush, walking back and forth. When she reached a floodplain, she saw in it a monster. This moved in a disgusting way and screaming horrifyingly. She was astonished and went to speak with the captain's son named Baltasar Ferreira and told him the case. But he did not believe her story. He asked her to come back and check if she had not been wrong. The Indian obeyed and came back even more frightened. Then Baltasar took a sword and went to check that it was some ounce or other animal of the earth. Looking from the same spot as India was, he saw a figure, but he was not sure what it was, for darkness covered the earth. As he got closer, he saw him better and realized that it was a marine animal. The monster then headed for the sea. Before he reached the waters, Baltasar gasped at the passage. The man hit him in the belly and the monster tried to fight back falling in the place where he was. He escaped from the crush, but not from the blood of the wound that gushed out and almost blinded him. The wounded monster advanced with gritted mouths and teeth. Baltasar then gave him a deep blow to the head. The monster was then almost dead. A few slaves appeared, alarmed by the cries of the Indian who witnessed everything. They took the monster and took it to the village where it was exposed to the sight of everyone. Never before has anything like this been seen on Brazilian soil.

Jurupari

Ceuci was a beautiful Indian woman who had gone out for a walk in the country in order to rest her mind from her worries. She walked for a long time and upon arriving in a colorful orchard, she rested in the shade of a tree. Upon waking up hungry, she ate one of her fruits called Mapati. This fruit was forbidden to girls who were in the fertile time. It happened that the juice of the fruit flowed down her body and reached her thighs, fecundating her. Her fellow villagers became aware of the fact and the council of elders decided to punish her with exile. In a land far away, she had her son. This child was called Jurupari and, according to belief, was sent from the Sun God. Jurupari's mission was to reshape the customs of men and find love. With only seven days to live, he appeared to be ten years old and possessed much wisdom. He taught others the will of the sun God. For this reason, he was also called a legislator.

Jurupari grew in wisdom, stature, and power. He further expanded his action by teaching and admonishing various communities. He brought the message of a new time filled with achievement, success and happiness for all. Inevitably, his actions went against the interest of some who plotted against him. They accused him of sorcerer gathering evidence and false witnesses. The son of the sun was then arrested, scourged and burned. But his message did not fade away, his memory lingering for a long time in the Indian daily life, being partially erased by the colonization that made him a demonic symbol.

Legend of the weed

Formerly, there was a nomadic indigenous tribe and at one point, they stopped in the vicinity of the source of the Tabay River. On his way back, an old Indian and his daughter were taken refuge in the jungle. Several days went by without anything-special happening until a strange-looking man appeared in the hiding place and dressed in odd clothes. The elderly offered the visitor a roast beef acuti (a local rodent) and a plate of tambu, a kind of larva snack. According to legend, this special visitor was an envoy of the forces of good. Being well received, in the form of retribution, he gave birth to a new plant in the middle of the forest, which was called Yari. From there the new plant grew offering leaves and twigs to prepare the mate.

The Legend of Victory-Regia

In a long time ago, in a distant Indian tribe, the moon (Jaci) at the dawn of the night caressed the faces of the Indian virgins of the village. By hiding behind the mountains, she chose the girls she liked most and turned them into stars in the sky. One of these girls, the warrior Naiá, dreamed of this encounter and the possible rapture. Even with all the advice of the elders, she remained irreducible in her purpose. No one could change her mind and every night she wanders the mountains for the moon. But she never reached her.

Time passed and she stood firm in her dream. It came to such an extent that she neither ate nor drank more. One day, as she rested by a lake, she saw the image of her Goddess reflected in the waters. Blinded by her desire, she dived into the water and sank. It was there that the moon sensitized by her effort resolved to reward it and transformed it into a "Star of the waters" that today is known as victory-regal. Thus, was born a beautiful plant.

Maira

One day came down from heaven an enigmatic being, cunning, wise and powerful. He was called Maira and could walk on the water, leave traces on the stones and teach many things to us. When he fulfilled his purpose, he returned to heaven promising his eternal blessing. It is also known as Nhanderequei or Karú-Sakaibê.

Pombero

The pombero is a forest spirit entrusted with caring for animals and nature in general. He can either be a friend or an enemy to people depending on how they act. Being a friend. He assists in hunting and in the search for food provided that in the right measure. If he is an enemy, he promotes accidents and discord in the house.

His name should never be pronounced aloud because it can cause irritation in him. Nor should you forget the renewal of your offerings for those who have already asked his for favors. Otherwise, evil will fall upon your house. It is quite worshiped in the region of Paraguay.

Pytajovái
Pytajovái is the spirit of war that fills our bravest warriors. Through its force, we are able to face the cruelest enemies in the name of what we believe. Even because life without honor is the same as nothing.

Saci pereré
Saci pereré is a dark boy with only one leg who can act for good and be playful. He uses a pipe and a red cap. This mythological being lives in such mischief as scaring off horses, producing accidents or tormenting people.

He manifests itself in a whirlwind of wind, leaves, and is captured if we cast a rosary in the boiling spot. Other interesting features are: Taking the hood, you get a wish; if someone is chased by him, he must play Laces because he will stop to untie the nodes allowing the escape. There is a rumor that it is said that the caipora is his father.

Legend of Tamandaré
Tamandaré is the ascendant of the Tupinambás and his brother Aricute the ascendant of the Tomimis. These two brothers lived in a village. The former was intelligent and wise while the second reckless, clumsy and impulsive. Once Aricute put the entire village in danger because of his behavior. It was there that Tamandaré hit with his foot on the ground causing a stream of water that flooded the whole place. Those who escaped the flood were Tamandaré and his wife climbing on a palm tree and his brother with his wife who climbed a jenipapeiro. Both of them fed on the fruits of the plants. When the water withdrew, they descended from the trees; they separated and repopulated the land.

The creation according to the Guarani mythology

Behold, Tupan lives from everlasting and is the maker of all things. By their will, the moon and the sun were created and with their help, Tupã descended the earth in the region known as Areguá, in Paraguay. From this place, he created everything that exists on the face of the earth besides fixing the stars in the sky. The man was the first created being formed from clay and the woman being a mixture of various elements of nature. Then Tupã God blew them up by giving life in abundance and free will.

The first humans were called Rupave and Sypave whose names respectively mean: Father of the peoples and mother of the peoples. They had three sons and several daughters. The eldest son was called Tumé Arandu considered the great prophet of the Guarani people. The second son was called Marangatu, a born leader, kind and understanding. He was the father of Kerana, the mother of the seven legendary monsters of the Guarani myth. Already the third son named Japeusá was a liar, arrogant, cheating, false, wanting to take advantage of the goodness of others. He committed suicide by being resurrected as a crab and from there all of the species were cursed having to walk backwards.

About the daughters, stood out Porásý, that sacrificed its own life to save one of the seven legendary monsters taking the power of the evil as a whole. Both sons and daughters have become important in one way or another leaving a legacy for future generations.

The seven legendary monsters

Behold, the spirit of the evil called Tau espoused kerana, the daughter of Marangatu, and together they had seven sons. The children were cursed by the Goddess Arasy, and except for one, they were all born as horrifying monsters. These seven are considered primary beings of the indigenous mythology being kept until today in the legends. Below are briefly described each of them.

Teju jagua is a God of the grottos, caves and lakes. His body is similar to that of a lizard with seven dog heads. Their basic food consists of fruits and honey. In his head, there is a gem. He lives in Jarau in the midst of a great treasure.

Mboi tu'i presents himself as a great snake with a parrot-beak and red tongue. He has scaly snakeskin and feathers on the head. He is the protector of amphibians, aquatic animals and wetlands.

Moñai is presented with two horns, which act as orientation. It dominates the open fields, being able to climb mountains and trees, which make it easier to obtain food. He is the typical thief in disguise, which provoked discord in the surrounding villages. But one fine day, when he was discovered, the inhabitants gathered to put an end to their actions. Porâsý then offered to help. She convinced Moñai of his love, but before marrying, he asked to meet his brothers. Moñai granted him the request and went in search of his brothers.

It was then prepared the wedding party to be held in the cave and the girl took the opportunity to get everyone drunk. Porâsý tried to escape, but without success. That is when she screamed and asked people to set fire to the cave with her inside. Her request was fulfilled and on account of her sacrifice she was transformed by the Gods into an intense point of light.

Jaci Jaterê is the only one of the brothers not to have a monster appearance. He appears generally as a man of short stature, handsome, slender, blue eyes carrying a magic staff. He is the protector of the weed, of the hidden treasures and lord of the naps.

Kurupi is a Guarani God who inhabits the dense forests and leaves at night with a full moon to torment men and animals. With low stature, yellow color, black eyes and sharp teeth moves through heels and is very fast. His favorite food are the animal's cub and feces of agouti.

Known for sarcastic laughter and being very smart and active, he is feared by the entire indigenous community. His main habitat is the Amazon jungle region. However, his influence is widespread in all peoples.

Ao is a terrible creature similar to the ram having sharp tusks. Its name derives from the sound that it causes when chasing its victims. He is considered the principle of fertility and his children are considered lords and protectors of the mountains.

Usually he is a cannibal-devourer of people not giving up easily to reach their victims. According to the myth, he also kidnaps children by taking them in front of his brother Jaci Jaterê.

Luison is a creature that has power over death. His physical appearance resembles a red-eyed monkey, with fish fins and a large phallus. His name comes from Werewolf. According to legend, a curse fell on him that is transmitted by his parents: On a full moon night, he turns into a half-dog and half-man creature.

The Xukuru people

"Well, that's what I learned from the ancients about Tupi-Guarani mythology. What did you think? (Juraci)

"A great knowledge. (The Seer)

"An important cultural rescue. (Emanuel)

"An adventure. Now could you tell a little of your people? (Messias)

"Of course. It all began when the Portuguese arrived in the region around 1654. The Portuguese crown donated land lots for foreigners for livestock purposes and thus remained for some time. In 1661, was founded the village of Ararobá of Our lady in the mountain. From there, indigenous slave labor began. A little more than a century later, in 1762, Ararobá became a village. The economy at this time revolved around the cultivation of maize, cassava, beans and livestock. It was also at this time that the invasions of our land began on behalf of the tenants. Over time, more invasions occurred taking land right from us. With the enactment of the land law in 1850, the invaders requested the government to extinguish the Xukuru settlement claiming that there were Indians that are no more legitimate. In response to requests, the empire decreed officially the extinction of the village in 1879. A year later, the county seat was transferred to Pesqueira. At this time, the Indians were very persecuted abandoning their dwelling and dispersing throughout the region. We begin to lose some of our identity there.

A few isolated Indians remained in hard-to-reach places, and others continued to be exploited by wealthy farmers. One thing that did not change was the claw of my people, the few who remained, remained faithful to their traditions involving religion, customs, teachings, values and vision of life. We survived with great pride. At the beginning of the 20th century, my people and other groups began a mobilization in search of land tenure and guarantee of their rights. We had to put pressure on the authorities that remained without concrete actions. Throughout the century, some actions were taken, such as reports and official implementation of the IPS (Indian Protection Service). However, conflicts with the ranchers remained. It is only after the 1988 constitution that we rekindle our hopes of having what is ours by right. Today we live scattered in twenty-four village by the mountain and in some parts of the county seat. (Juraci)

"How beautiful. I'm proud of you, my friend. (Messias)

"What a wonderful story. (The Seer)

"I'm delighted. (Emanuel)

"Thank you all. Much more beautiful is the story of a person I will tell you from now on:

PART II

Back from exile

We were in the early 70's, precisely in the village of Cimbres belonging to Pesqueira-PE. It was the moment when I returned from exile and rediscovered my relatives of the Xukuru tribe. I still had mother, siblings, cousins and nephews. All were good people who despite the influence of the white man remained faithful to their origins. It was what we had left after the oppression of the moments lived.

The first thing I did upon my arrival was to rescue my house, my position in the tribe, to meet acquaintances and try to raise my life. The experience in Ibimirim showed me a horrible face of the human being who only worries about assaulting, humiliating and taking advantage of the situation of others. From that moment, I had to recover my self-esteem by affirming to myself that I was capable. I only had this choice.

It was thinking of this that in the language of white I met a good person, got married and made a family. I had two sons, a man and a woman named Jupi and Serena respectively. Modesty aside, the two were very nice and beautiful. As soon as they began to take their first steps, my wife and I became involved in their creation. Even if parents say their love for their children is the same, it is not true. I declare that my favorite was Serena and it is upon her that my narrative will stop.

Family on the river

One of the first community leisure activities with our children was the ride to the Cimbres river on the south side of the community. My family and others would occasionally go to bathe and fish in it. This was the first time with our small children, which in a way was special.

My wife and I focused on fishing and bathing while our children played with other children. Everything was very beautiful: moderate climate, blue sky, winds blowing from both sides, the joy was general. To be there was to be in a paradise full of treasures.

The day went by and we had the opportunity to teach our children the love and power of Mother Nature, to be like the flowing river delivered to their destination. Respect and tranquility prevailed all the time.

One critical moment was when my lovely Serena nearly drowned due to our carelessness. The fate of it is that a friend saw everything and rushed to save her. Thank you so much and we will charge more. After all, our children were our responsibility.

In addition, everything went well. At the end of the afternoon, we returned to the village and went to sleep with a clear conscience. Our children had taken the first step toward discovering the world. This was a great feat for owl fathers like us.

Birthday

Our community often hosts parties on important dates. The fifth anniversary of Serena and other children was a reason to organize a special event involving all of the tribe and friends.

It was the month of March 1975, a sunny Monday and hectic fair. Using our instruments, we chant a joyful melody, sing, dance, practice sports and challenges, as well as cherish our children. Everything was very beautiful and inviting leading us to a good reflection on our future and the community. We had the great joy and responsibility of leading these little ones. What we wanted to show them was the values of our people so that when they were bigger, they made the difference in a contextualized society. The world needs good, prepared souls.

In the end, we did a ritual of preparation and blessed them. From there the adventure would continue with even greater care. It was our duty.

In school

At the beginning of the year 1976, we enrolled our children in the school of our community. Taking good luggage from home, they have shown themselves to be exemplary in behavior in this social environment. Serena stood out among all for being applied, intelligent, understanding and have team spirit. Already Jupi was a little relaxed and this caused me anguish. I soon felt that he would not have as much progress as his sister.

At that time, the school in our village had only primary education so that as they advanced in degree they had to go to other schools. They completed elementary education in Cimbres and high school in Pesqueira. Jupi dropped out of school and while Serena passed a municipal competition as a teacher. It was the first great achievement of my little baby that made me very proud.

This time of teaching and learning was very rich for my daughter, conquering friendships, knowledge, recognition, fun and independence.

She was almost a grown woman, and this caused me apprehension and contentment concomitantly.

The feast of the patron saint

Due to the professional duties, Serena moved to Pesqueira where the economy and events of the region were concentrated. She always visited us on weekends. I had total confidence in her character and therefore I allowed her to leave. Because we do not own our children. They belong to the world.

An event that was marked in our memories was the feast of our patroness, our lady of the mountains. Everything was wonderful: the singing, the dancing, the tourists, the drink, the forró, the reunion with friends and the new contacts. Among these new ones, we had a surprise: to meet the first boyfriend of our young woman whose name was Carlos. He was a tall, blond, strong, well-groomed, and kind man. I cannot lie that the fact that he did not belong to our ethnic group displeased me. However, with the passage of time and with the coexistence we learn to like him and to get involved. We even went out together for a cold beer. Carlos was a respected physician of our region, which proved that the love had no borders or prejudices.

This important moment brought me beautiful memories of our past. I was happy for my girl to be well, a girl I saw growing up full of problems, but confident in a good future. How many times have we not seen her disappoint with flirting, false friendships, betrayals and we always recommend being very careful? But we always made it clear that she needed to try to be happy. At that moment, everything seemed to be well trodden. But nothing was yet accomplished.

The phone call

It was a sunny Sunday in September of 1990. It was almost night when the chief warned us that there was a phone call from our daughter at the local post. We were rushed to attend and in doing so, on the other side, we heard the agonized voice of our daughter asking for help. At first, we asked her to calm down and try to tell us what was going on calmly.

The response we had was staggering: She had been raped and abandoned by her then boyfriend. We were in shock. How could such a nice person become such a monster? Appearances really deceived.

We asked our daughter to come home and when she arrived, we gave her every possible affection so that she could recover. With the license, she had taken from the city hall, she could then return to our company and try to raise her head. As for the criminal, our repulsion was enough. We could not face him because he was very influential in front of the authorities. An attitude against him would be useless.

The important thing now was to try to find a solution and a way. What had not changed was our convictions and our love for our children.

Change

Time has passed a little. Serena improved and returned to her studies. She passed with merit obtaining a scholarship to attend college in the capital. We were happy with this feat and we did not find it difficult for her to pursue her dreams.

In 1991, she had already settled in Recife. We know little what happened to her there due to lack of communication. In the meetings we had at the end of the year, we learned that she completed her degree in agronomy and specialization. We were delighted with the photos and their descriptions of how beautiful and acculturated the capital was. The last time we saw her, we were glad that she was getting married.

It was all a slight mistake. Months later, through the news published in a newspaper in the capital, we learned that she had been murdered by her then fiancé. It was an unexpected and overwhelming pain in our lives. Serena had definitely not been born to be happy and the cause had been the violence of the whites.

Now all we had left was Jupi who, to our good fortune, had become an important man. But the memory of our warrior would never run away. My eternal love is with her somewhere.

Farewell

"I appreciate sharing an important part of your life. We are honored. (The Seer)

"I am sorry for what happened. (Emanuel)

"Trust is only given to friends. Thank you for considering us as such. (Messias)

"I appreciate everyone's words. My mission is completed here. I hope you have taken great advantage and are prepared to take a new vision of life from now on. (Juraci)

"It was very good. We are others thanks to you. We will continue our journey remembering your figure forever. (The Seer)

"So be it. (Juraci)

"Bye. (The seer, Emanuel and Messiah)

"See you. (Juraci)

The Sons of Light series crew set off home. The short trip to Cimbres is covered with a good sense of mission accomplished, recovering the culture of true Brazilians. When they arrive to the village, they take a stocking until the seat of the municipality. From there, the seer goes to little Mimoso and the others return to the region of Ibimirim. They would wait for the opportunity of new adventures that would surely bring even more surprises. Until the next book, readers.

END

www.ingramcontent.com/pod-product-compliance
Lightning Source LLC
LaVergne TN
LVHW010559070526
838199LV00063BA/5019